DISNEY · PIXAR

ONWARD

Tales of the Manticore

The Wizard, the Bard, and the Manager

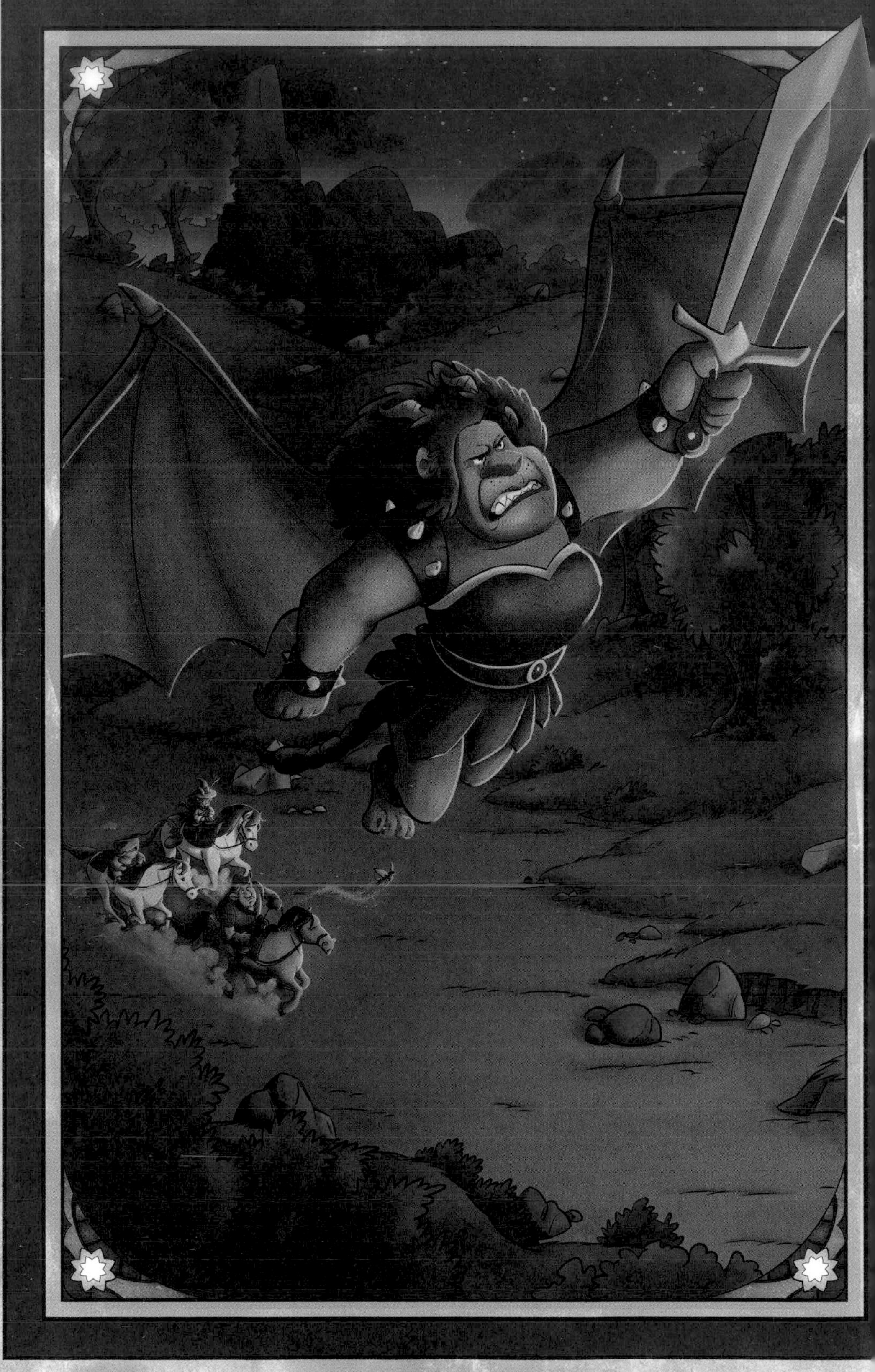

DISNEY · PIXAR
ONWARD

Tales of the Manticore
The Wizard, the Bard, and the Manager

Written by
MARIKO TAMAKI and **DAN SCANLON**

Art by
**ARIANNA FLOREAN, DENNY MINONNE,
FERRAN RODRIGUEZ, IVAN NIKULIN,**
and **MARIO DEL PENNINO**

Colors by
IVAN SHAVRIN

Letters by
JIMMY BETANCOURT OF COMICRAFT

Cover by
DENNY MINONNE with **IVAN SHAVRIN**

DARK HORSE BOOKS

DARK HORSE BOOKS

PRESIDENT AND PUBLISHER MIKE RICHARDSON

EDITORS SHANTEL LaROCQUE AND BRETT ISRAEL

DESIGNER JEN EDWARDS   DIGITAL ART TECHNICIAN JOSIE CHRISTENSEN

NEIL HANKERSON Executive Vice President • TOM WEDDLE Chief Financial Officer • RANDY STRADLEY Vice President of Publishing • NICK McWHORTER Chief Business Development Officer • DALE LaFOUNTAIN Chief Information Officer • MATT PARKINSON Vice President of Marketing • VANESSA TODD-HOLMES Vice President of Production and Scheduling • MARK BERNARDI Vice President of Book Trade and Digital Sales • KEN LIZZI General Counsel • DAVE MARSHALL Editor in Chief • DAVEY ESTRADA Editorial Director • CHRIS WARNER Senior Books Editor • CARY GRAZZINI Director of Specialty Projects • LIA RIBACCHI Art Director • MATT DRYER Director of Digital Art and Prepress • MICHAEL GOMBOS Senior Director of Licensed Publications • KARI YADRO Director of Custom Programs • KARI TORSON Director of International Licensing • SEAN BRICE Director of Trade Sales

DISNEY PUBLISHING WORLDWIDE GLOBAL MAGAZINES, COMICS AND PARTWORKS

PUBLISHER Lynn Waggoner • EDITORIAL TEAM Bianca Coletti (Director, Magazines), Guido Frazzini (Director, Comics), Carlotta Quattrocolo (Executive Editor), Stefano Ambrosio (Executive Editor, New IP), Camilla Vedove (Senior Manager, Editorial Development), Behnoosh Khalili (Senior Editor), Julie Dorris (Senior Editor), Mina Riazi (Assistant Editor), Gabriela Capasso (Assistant Editor) • DESIGN Enrico Soave (Senior Designer) • ART Ken Shue (VP, Global Art), Manny Mederos (Senior Illustration Manager, Comics and Magazines), Roberto Santillo (Creative Director), Marco Ghiglione (Creative Manager), Stefano Attardi (Illustration Manager) • PORTFOLIO MANAGEMENT Olivia Ciancarelli (Director) • BUSINESS & MARKETING Mariantonietta Galla (Senior Manager, Franchise), Virpi Korhonen (Editorial Manager)

Published by Dark Horse Books
A division of Dark Horse Comics LLC
10956 SE Main Street | Milwaukie, OR 97222

DarkHorse.com

To find a comics shop in your area, visit comicshoplocator.com

First edition: April 2020
eBook ISBN 978-1-50671-560-5
Trade Paperback ISBN 978-1-50671-551-3

1 3 5 7 9 10 8 6 4 2
Printed in Canada

FOREWORD
BY *ONWARD* FILM DIRECTOR DAN SCANLON

OVER THE LAST FEW YEARS I'VE BECOME A HUGE
COMIC BOOK FAN!

Every week, I look forward to going to my local comics store
and finding something new. I love movies, but there's something
about comics that make me more open to exploring genres that
I wouldn't necessarily try out in film. I guess because movies
demand a two-hour sitting commitment, and with comics you
can dip in and out at your leisure.

And though I love the shared experience of film, there's
something so personal about the experience a comic offers.
You decide the character's voice, you decide how the pictures
move. Comics are everything I love about visual mediums and
the written word combined into one art form.

So, when Disney, Pixar, and Dark Horse pitched the idea of
making a graphic novel set in the world of *Onward* I was
beyond excited. One, because I wanted to tell more stories in
the world we spent five years developing; and two, because
every time I grab a comic off the rack I feel such admiration
for anyone that's been a part of making one. I wanted to be a
part of making one as well.

Onward is a comedic film based on my own personal
experiences so I wanted the comic to have the same humor
and emotion. However, we wanted this to be its own unique
original story. So I totally geeked out when I found we were
able to get one of my favorite authors, Mariko Tamaki, to
write the comic! Mariko was perfect for this project because
her work spans from beautiful personal human character

pieces to thrilling high stakes action stories. She saw the movie once and immediately began to pitch ideas for the characters and storylines that became this book. It was endlessly inspiring to watch not only how quickly Mariko conjured whole scenes from thin air but also how flexible she was when other ideas were pitched in the room. I learned so much just seeing how she'd take an idea of mine and not only go with it, but make it stronger.

And as I mentioned, we also got to expand the world more in this book. There were characters and ideas in the movie that myself and the filmmaking team had to cut from the film because they weren't moving the story of Ian and Barley forward. Now we have a chance to feature some of those characters and locations in this story.

I hope you enjoy reading this book as much as I enjoyed watching its creation. It was a total comic book fantasy camp for me. A crash course from a great writer, great artists, editors, and publishers. Being the director of *Onward* I'm pretty sure I'll be given a few free copies of this book, but I can't wait to go to my local comic book store and buy a copy off the rack!

-DAN SCANLON
Director/co-writer of *Onward*

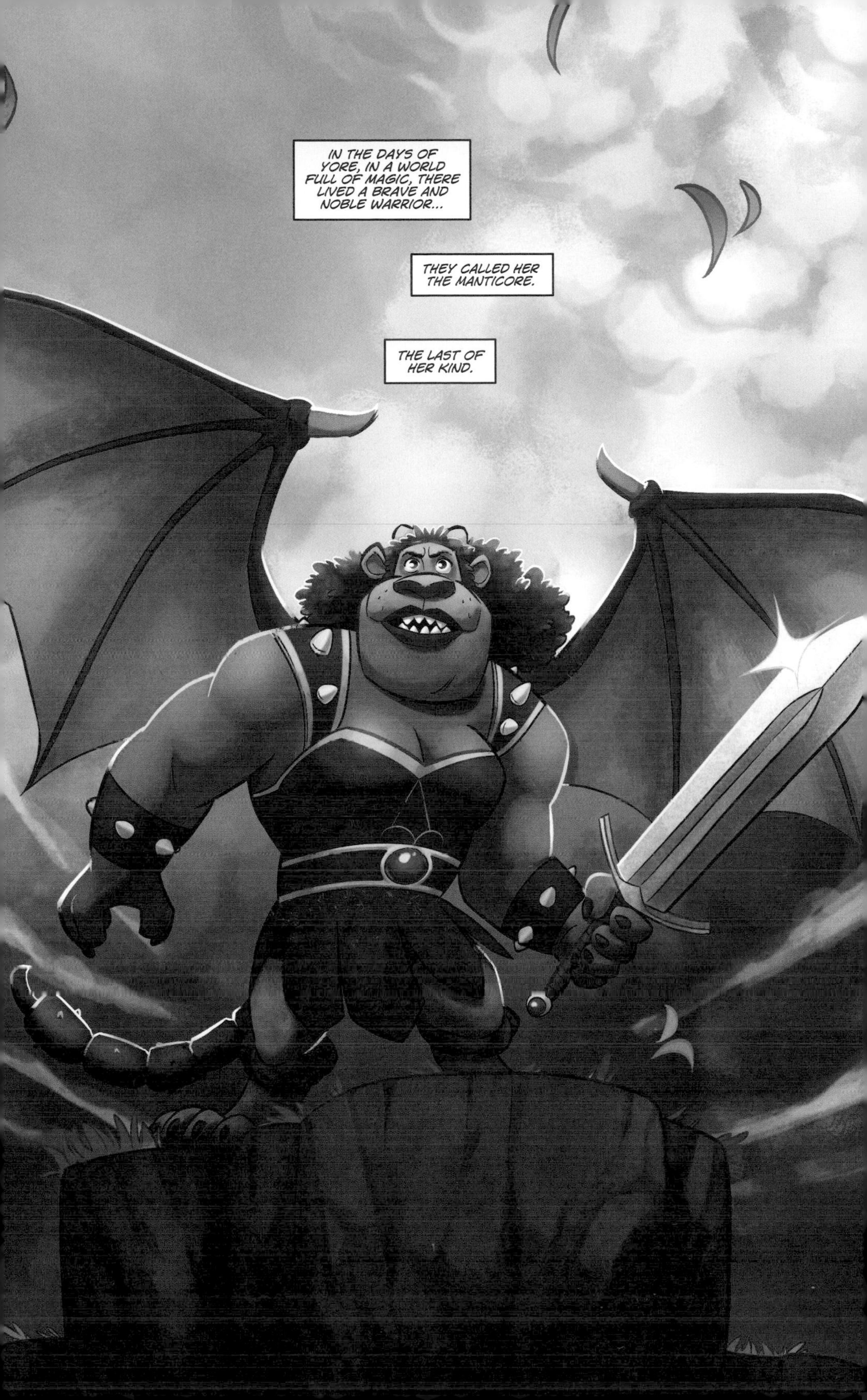
IN THE DAYS OF YORE, IN A WORLD FULL OF MAGIC, THERE LIVED A BRAVE AND NOBLE WARRIOR...
THEY CALLED HER THE MANTICORE.
THE LAST OF HER KIND.

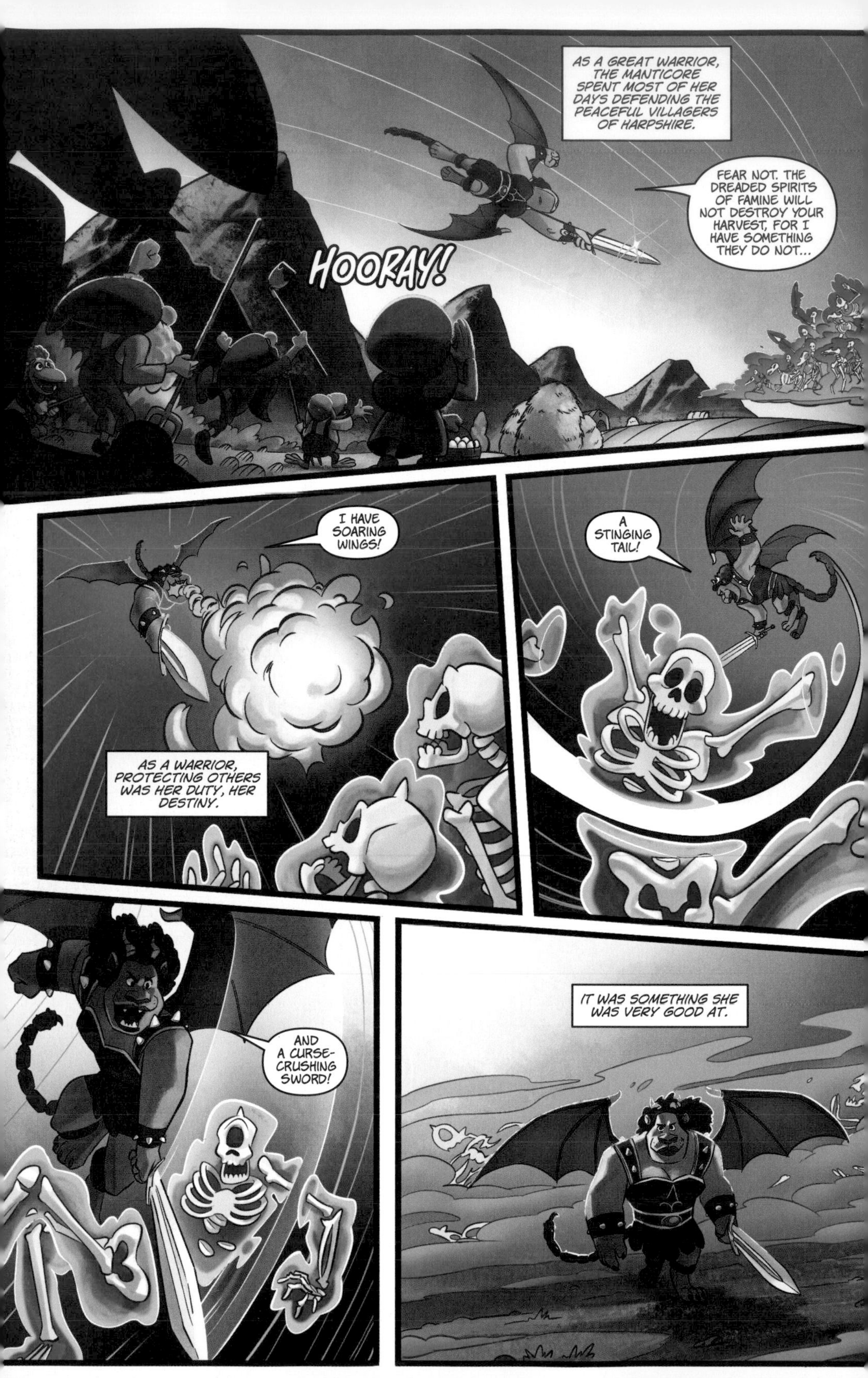
AS A GREAT WARRIOR, THE MANTICORE SPENT MOST OF HER DAYS DEFENDING THE PEACEFUL VILLAGERS OF HARPSHIRE.
FEAR NOT. THE DREADED SPIRITS OF FAMINE WILL NOT DESTROY YOUR HARVEST, FOR I HAVE SOMETHING THEY DO NOT...
HOORAY!
I HAVE SOARING WINGS!
AS A WARRIOR, PROTECTING OTHERS WAS HER DUTY, HER DESTINY.
A STINGING TAIL!
AND A CURSE-CRUSHING SWORD!
IT WAS SOMETHING SHE WAS VERY GOOD AT.

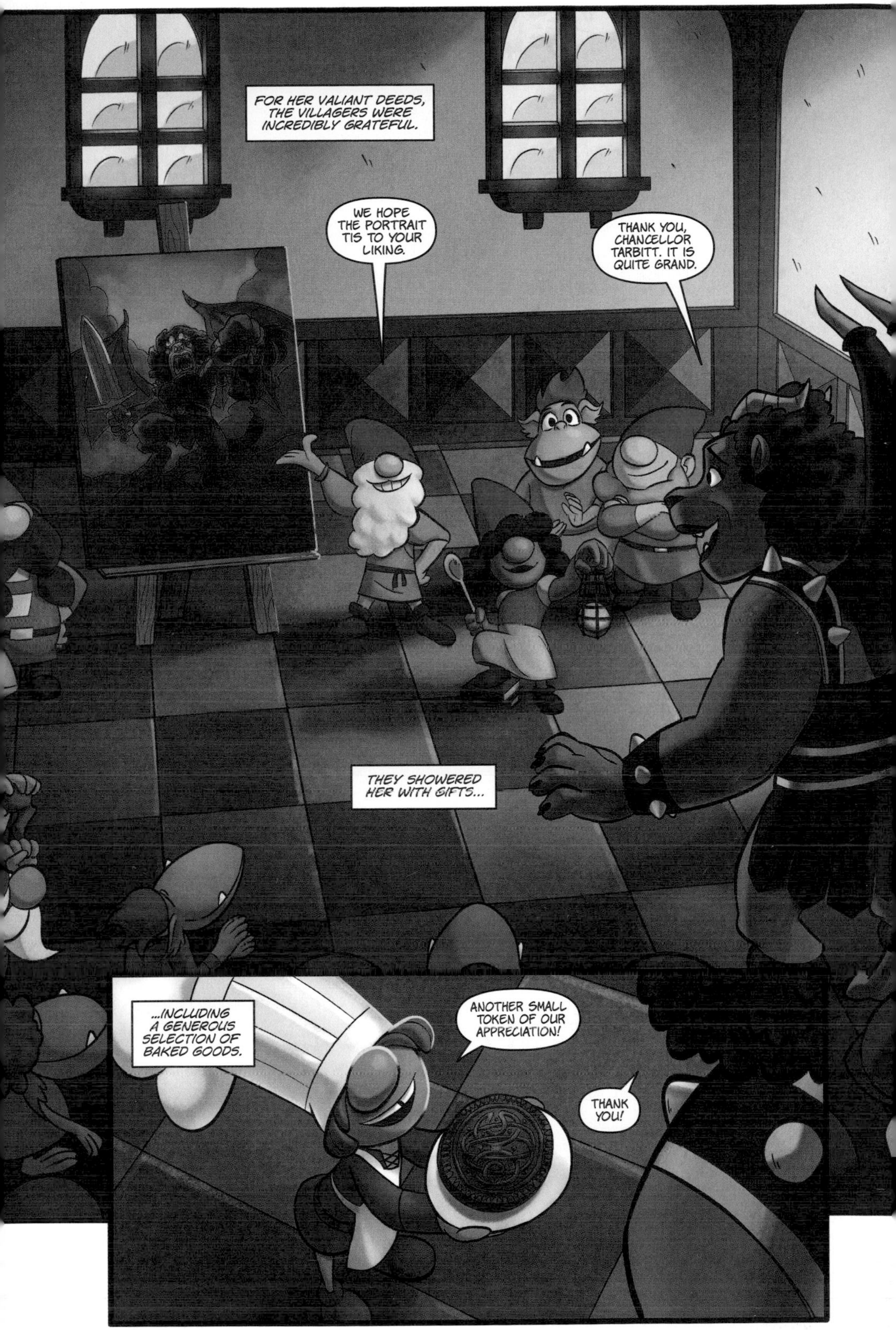
FOR HER VALIANT DEEDS, THE VILLAGERS WERE INCREDIBLY GRATEFUL.
WE HOPE THE PORTRAIT TIS TO YOUR LIKING.
THANK YOU, CHANCELLOR TARBITT. IT IS QUITE GRAND.
THEY SHOWERED HER WITH GIFTS...
...INCLUDING A GENEROUS SELECTION OF BAKED GOODS.
ANOTHER SMALL TOKEN OF OUR APPRECIATION!
THANK YOU!

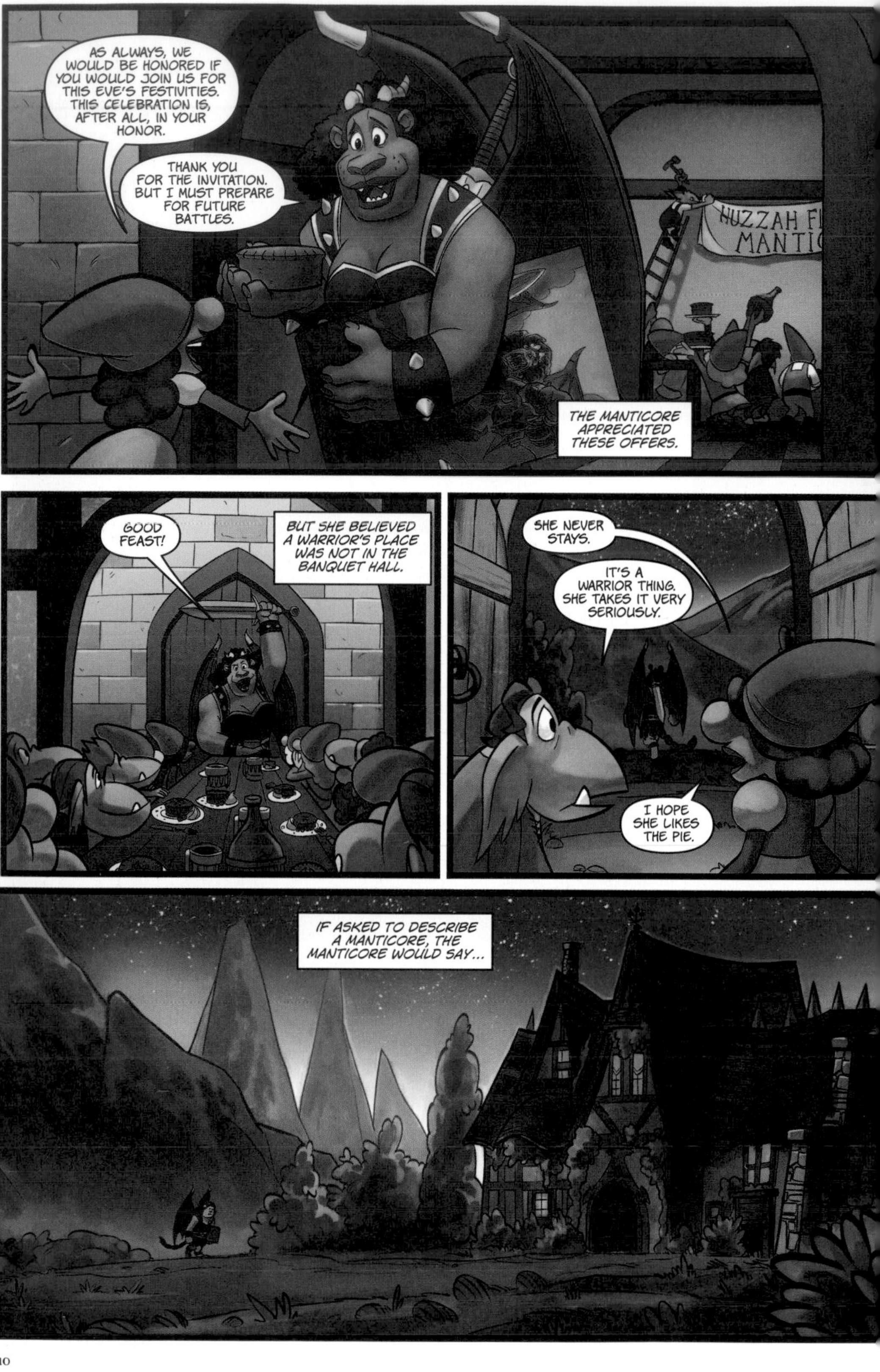
AS ALWAYS, WE WOULD BE HONORED IF YOU WOULD JOIN US FOR THIS EVE'S FESTIVITIES. THIS CELEBRATION IS, AFTER ALL, IN YOUR HONOR.
THANK YOU FOR THE INVITATION. BUT I MUST PREPARE FOR FUTURE BATTLES.
THE MANTICORE APPRECIATED THESE OFFERS.
GOOD FEAST!
BUT SHE BELIEVED A WARRIOR'S PLACE WAS NOT IN THE BANQUET HALL.
SHE NEVER STAYS.
IT'S A WARRIOR THING. SHE TAKES IT VERY SERIOUSLY.
I HOPE SHE LIKES THE PIE.
IF ASKED TO DESCRIBE A MANTICORE, THE MANTICORE WOULD SAY...

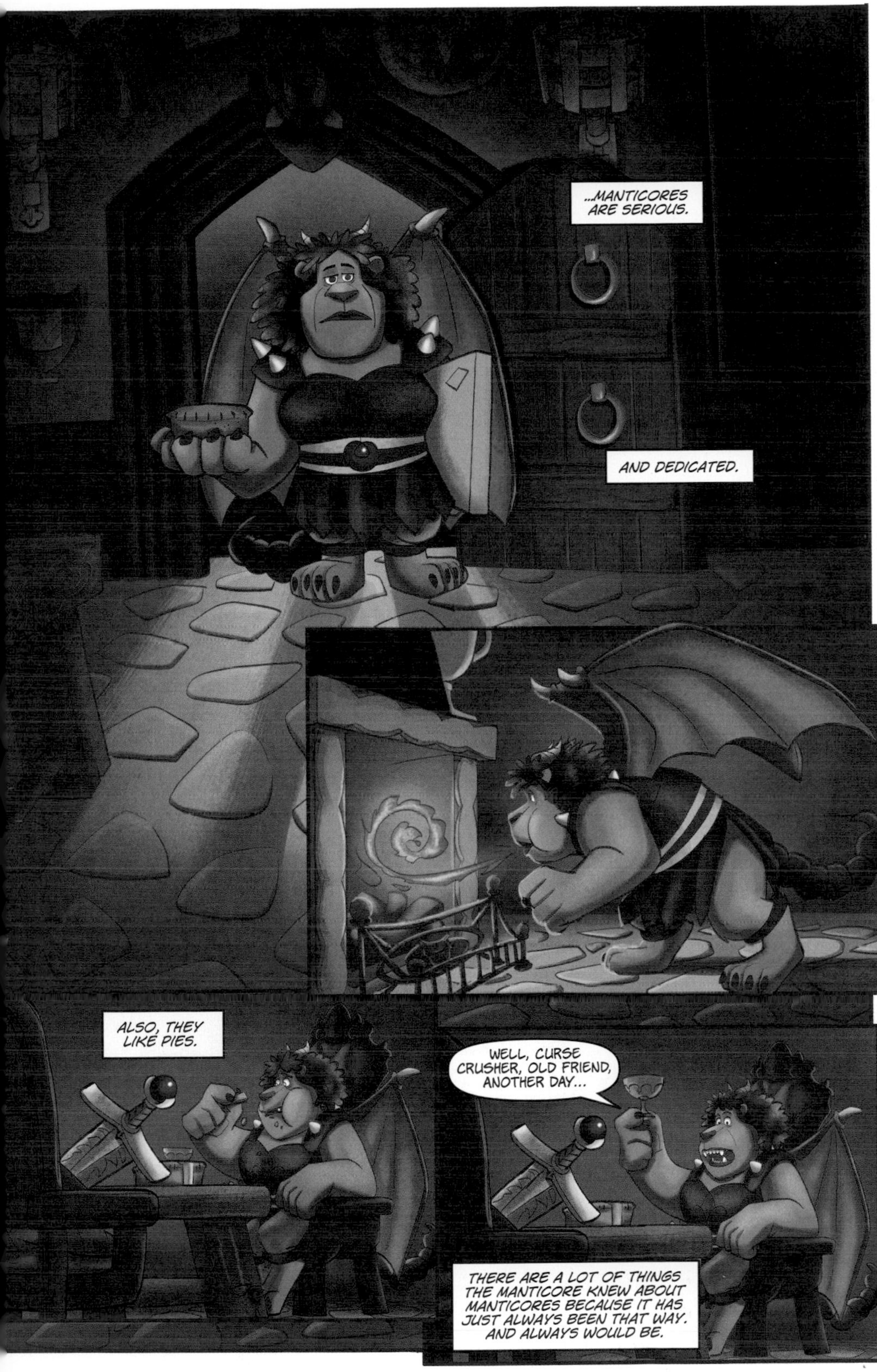
...MANTICORES ARE SERIOUS.
AND DEDICATED.
ALSO, THEY LIKE PIES.
WELL, CURSE CRUSHER, OLD FRIEND, ANOTHER DAY...
THERE ARE A LOT OF THINGS THE MANTICORE KNEW ABOUT MANTICORES BECAUSE IT HAS JUST ALWAYS BEEN THAT WAY. AND ALWAYS WOULD BE.

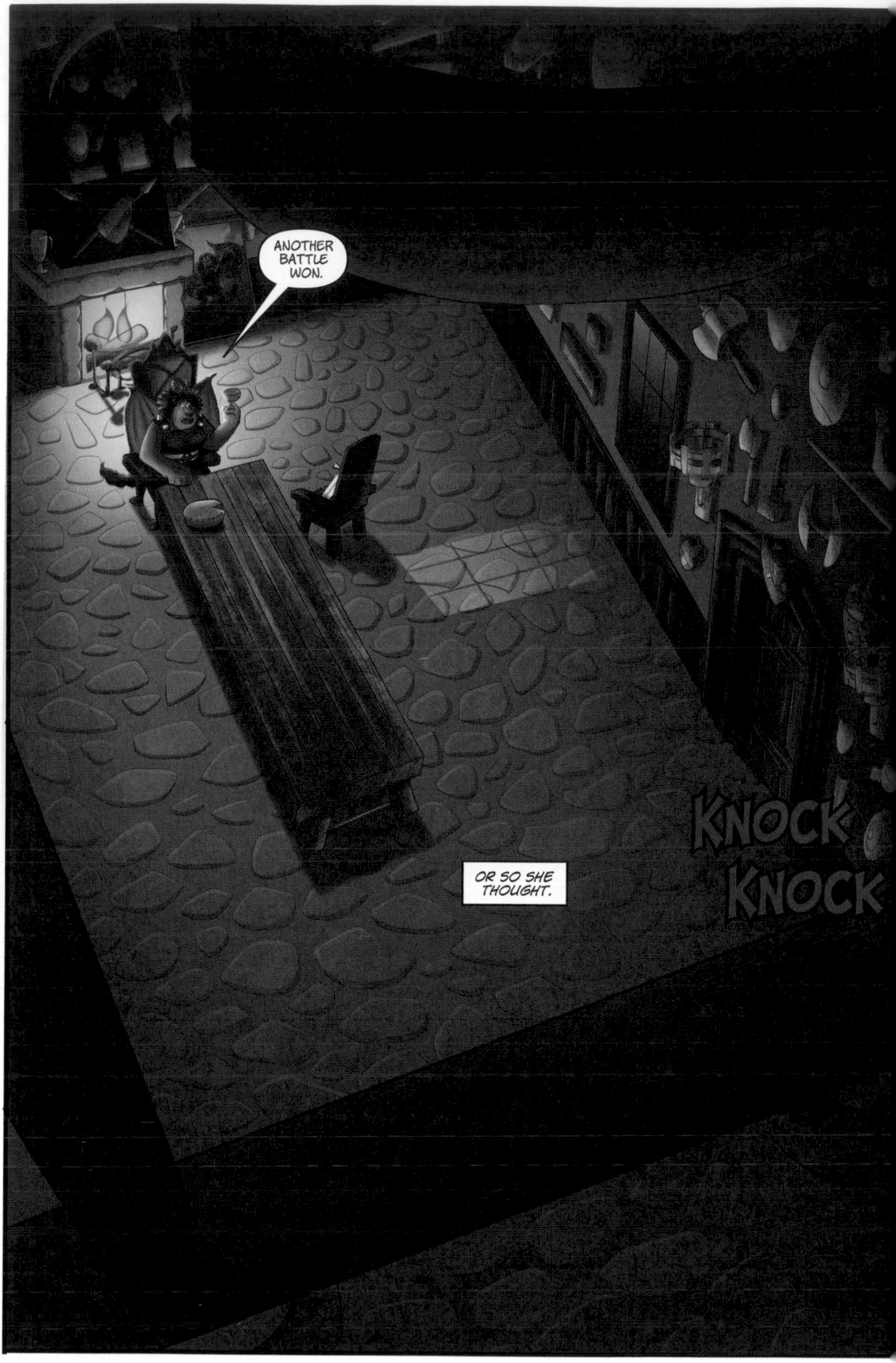
ANOTHER BATTLE WON.
OR SO SHE THOUGHT.
KNOCK KNOCK

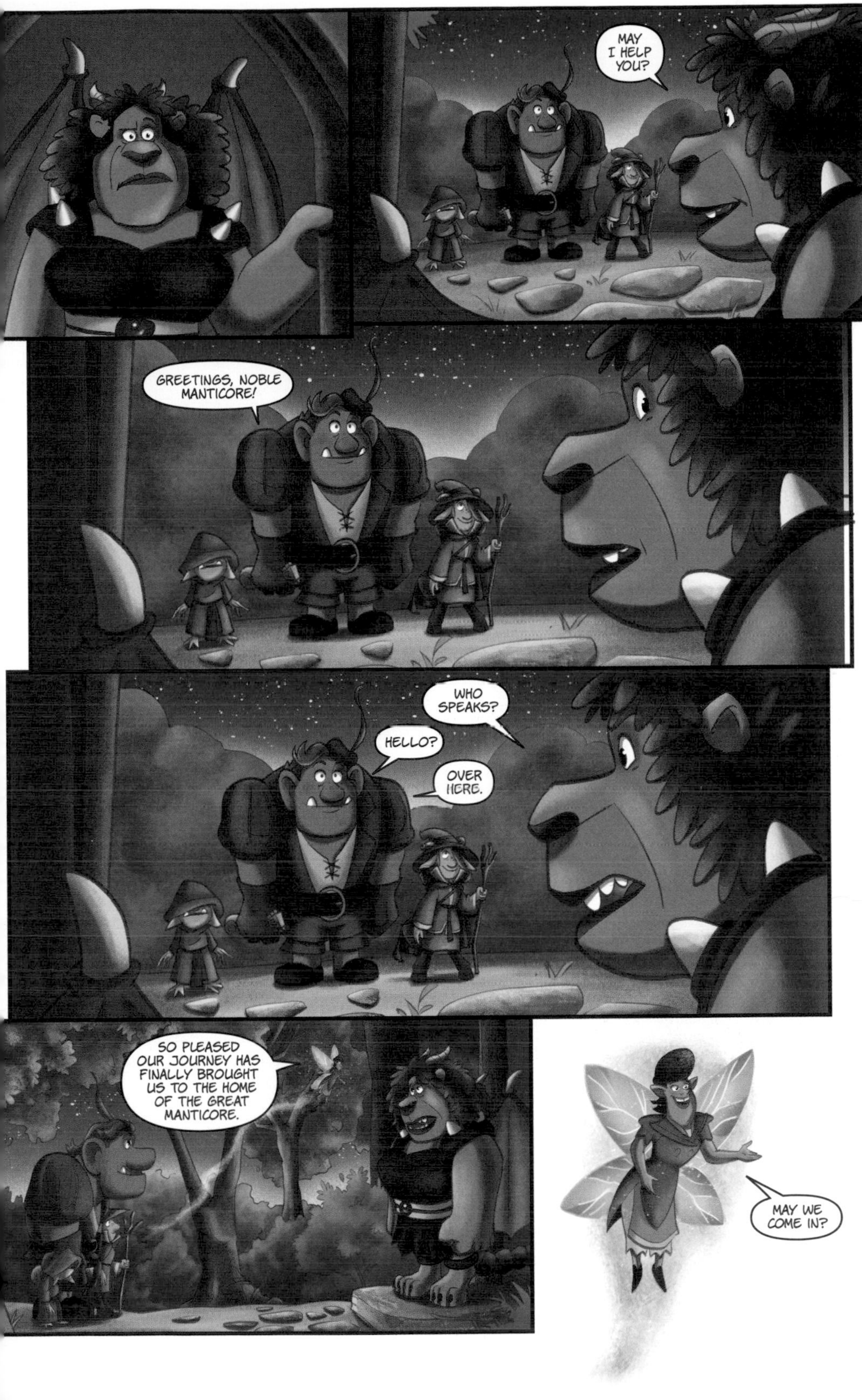
MAY I HELP YOU?
GREETINGS, NOBLE MANTICORE!
HELLO?
WHO SPEAKS?
OVER HERE.
SO PLEASED OUR JOURNEY HAS FINALLY BROUGHT US TO THE HOME OF THE GREAT MANTICORE.
MAY WE COME IN?

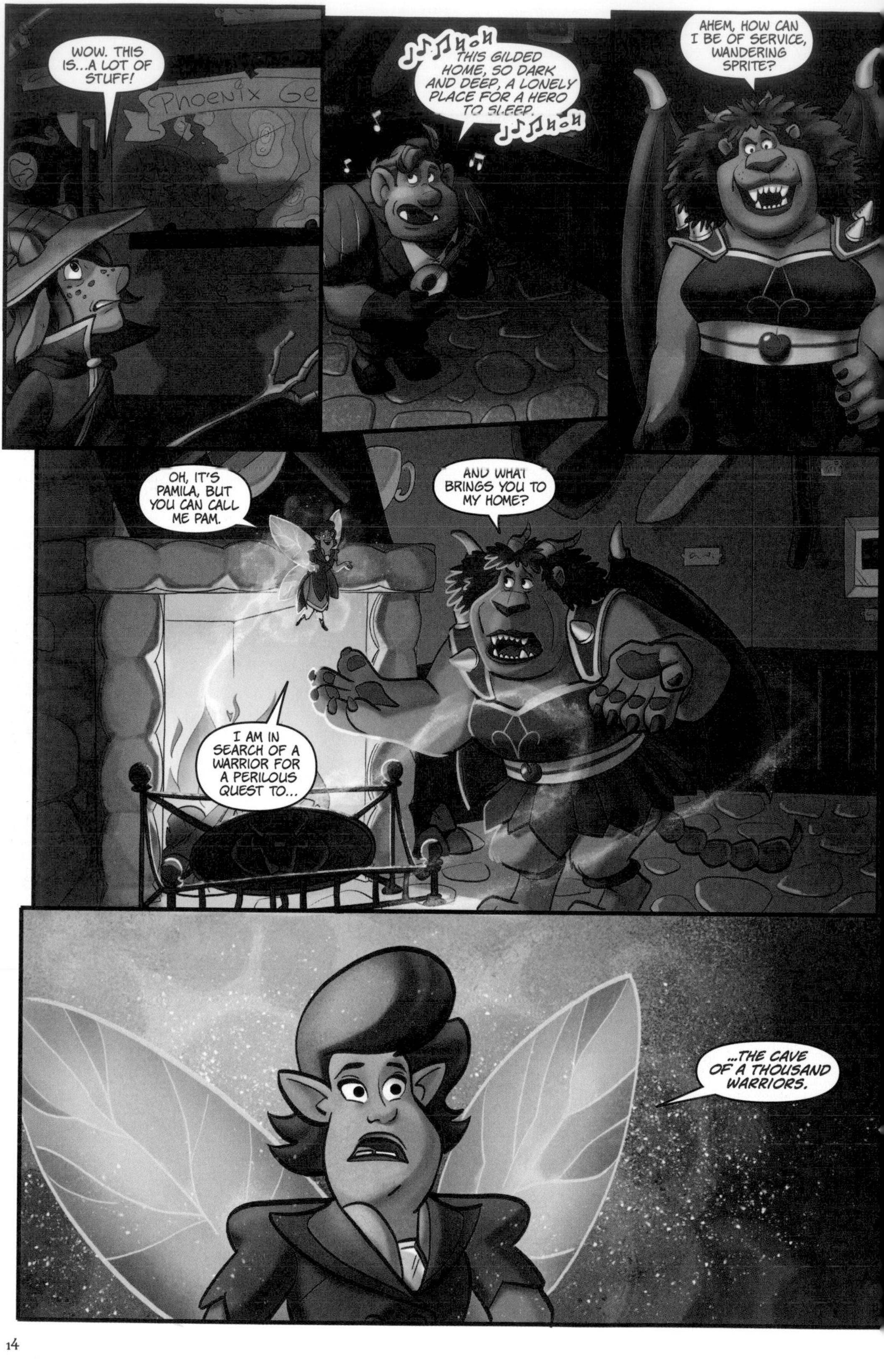
WOW. THIS IS...A LOT OF STUFF!
Phoenix Ge
THIS GILDED HOME, SO DARK AND DEEP, A LONELY PLACE FOR A HERO TO SLEEP.
AHEM, HOW CAN I BE OF SERVICE, WANDERING SPRITE?
OH, IT'S PAMILA, BUT YOU CAN CALL ME PAM.
AND WHAT BRINGS YOU TO MY HOME?
I AM IN SEARCH OF A WARRIOR FOR A PERILOUS QUEST TO...
...THE CAVE OF A THOUSAND WARRIORS.

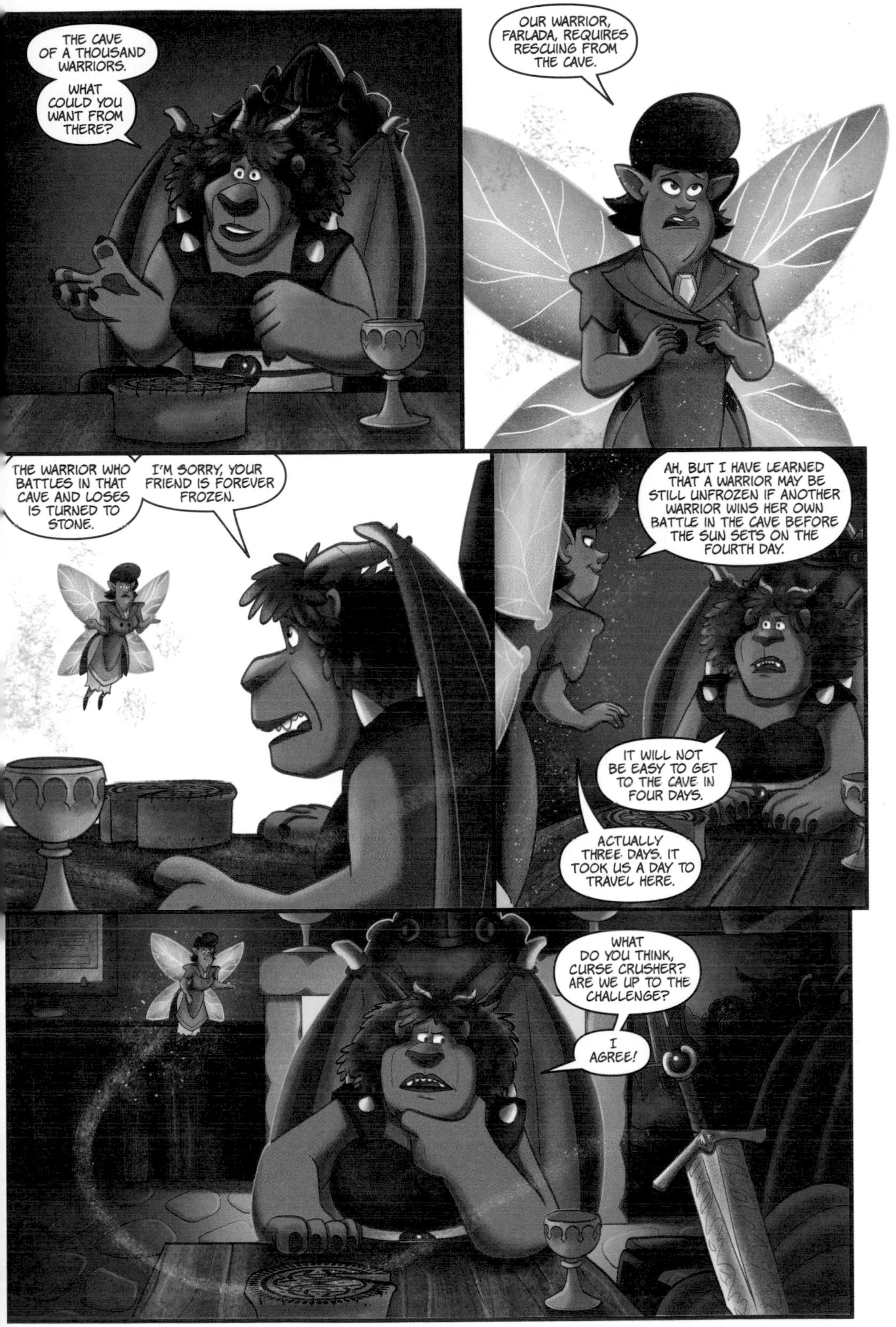
THE CAVE OF A THOUSAND WARRIORS.
WHAT COULD YOU WANT FROM THERE?
OUR WARRIOR, FARLADA, REQUIRES RESCUING FROM THE CAVE.
THE WARRIOR WHO BATTLES IN THAT CAVE AND LOSES IS TURNED TO STONE.
I'M SORRY, YOUR FRIEND IS FOREVER FROZEN.
AH, BUT I HAVE LEARNED THAT A WARRIOR MAY BE STILL UNFROZEN IF ANOTHER WARRIOR WINS HER OWN BATTLE IN THE CAVE BEFORE THE SUN SETS ON THE FOURTH DAY.
IT WILL NOT BE EASY TO GET TO THE CAVE IN FOUR DAYS.
ACTUALLY THREE DAYS. IT TOOK US A DAY TO TRAVEL HERE.
WHAT DO YOU THINK, CURSE CRUSHER? ARE WE UP TO THE CHALLENGE?
I AGREE!

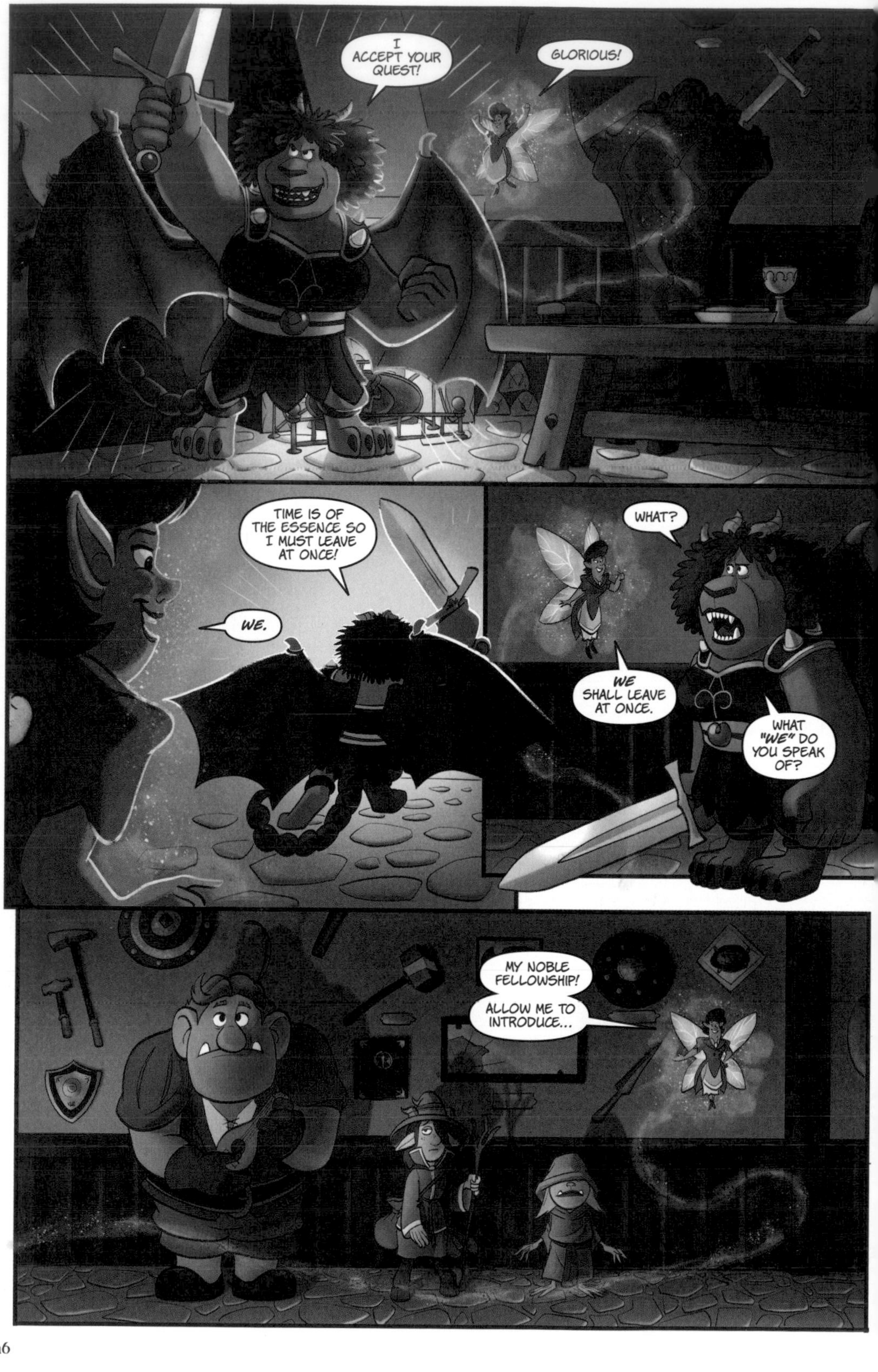
I ACCEPT YOUR QUEST!
GLORIOUS!
TIME IS OF THE ESSENCE SO I MUST LEAVE AT ONCE!
WE.
WHAT?
WE SHALL LEAVE AT ONCE.
WHAT "WE" DO YOU SPEAK OF?
MY NOBLE FELLOWSHIP!
ALLOW ME TO INTRODUCE...

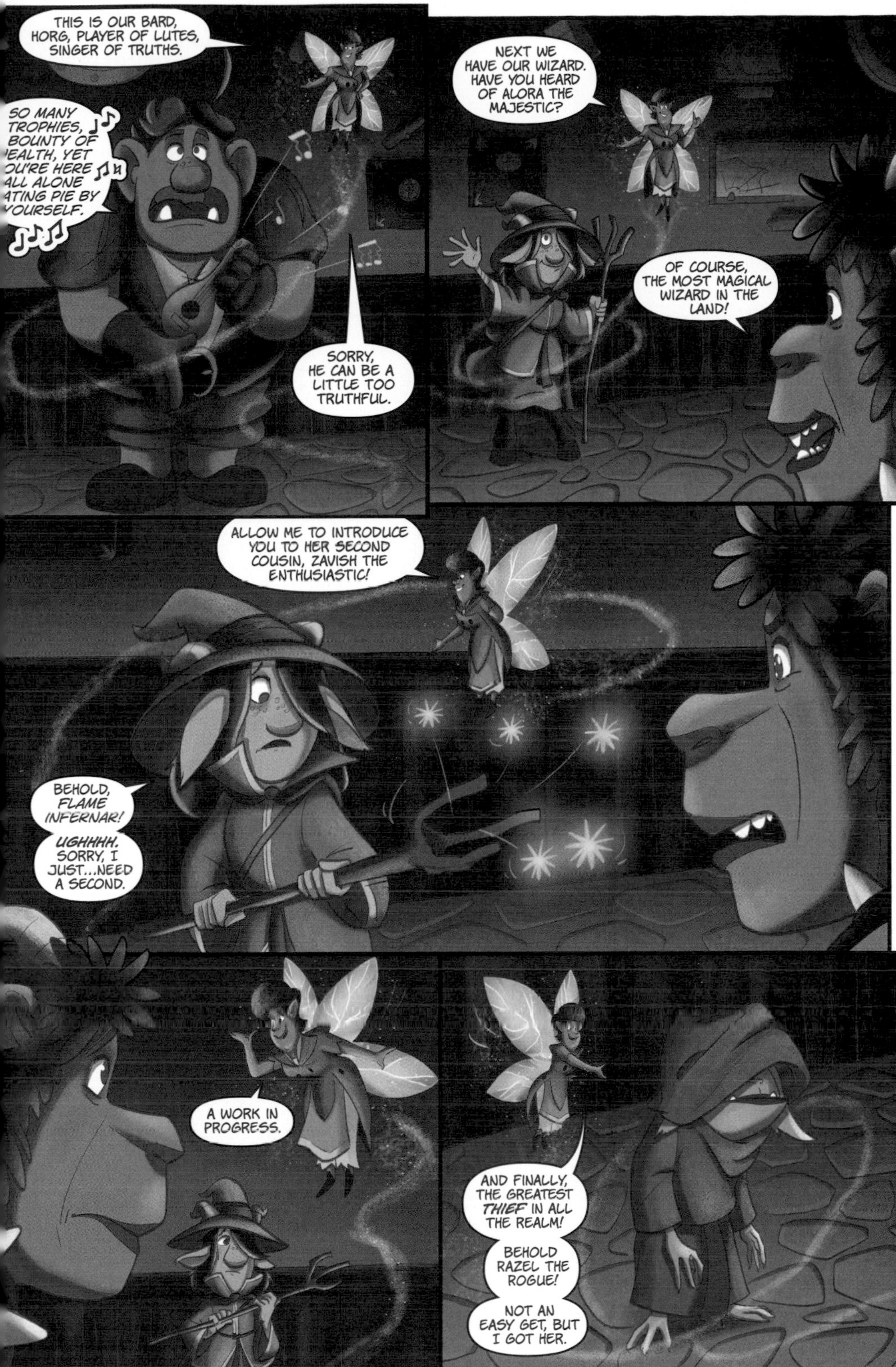
THIS IS OUR BARD, HORG, PLAYER OF LUTES, SINGER OF TRUTHS.
SO MANY TROPHIES, BOUNTY OF WEALTH, YET YOU'RE HERE ALL ALONE EATING PIE BY YOURSELF.
SORRY, HE CAN BE A LITTLE TOO TRUTHFUL.
NEXT WE HAVE OUR WIZARD. HAVE YOU HEARD OF ALORA THE MAJESTIC?
OF COURSE, THE MOST MAGICAL WIZARD IN THE LAND!
ALLOW ME TO INTRODUCE YOU TO HER SECOND COUSIN, ZAVISH THE ENTHUSIASTIC!
BEHOLD, *FLAME INFERNAR!*
UGHHHH. SORRY, I JUST...NEED A SECOND.
A WORK IN PROGRESS.
AND FINALLY, THE GREATEST *THIEF* IN ALL THE REALM!
BEHOLD RAZEL THE ROGUE!
NOT AN EASY GET, BUT I GOT HER.

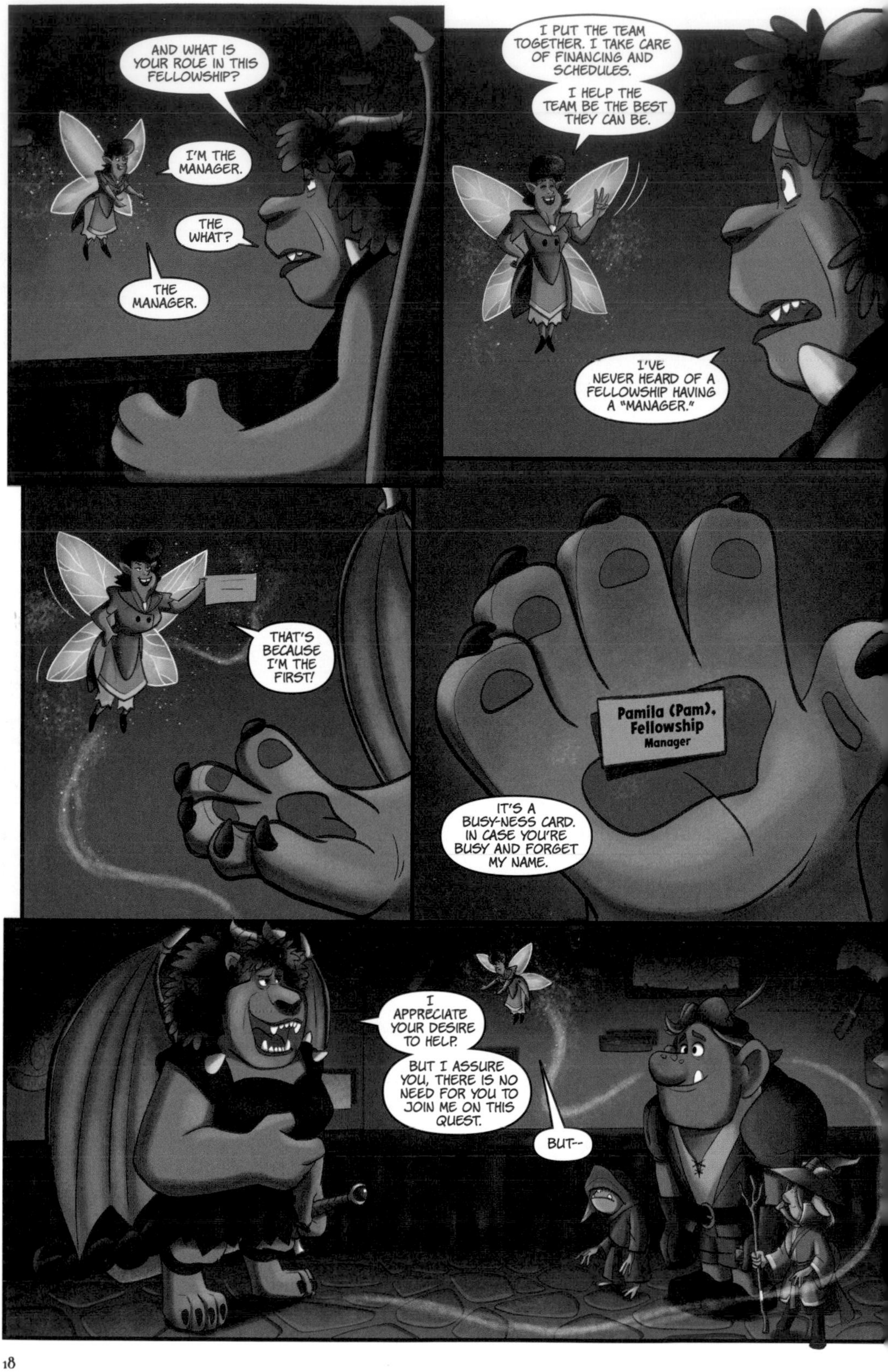
AND WHAT IS YOUR ROLE IN THIS FELLOWSHIP?
I'M THE MANAGER.
THE WHAT?
THE MANAGER.
I PUT THE TEAM TOGETHER. I TAKE CARE OF FINANCING AND SCHEDULES.
I HELP THE TEAM BE THE BEST THEY CAN BE.
I'VE NEVER HEARD OF A FELLOWSHIP HAVING A "MANAGER."
THAT'S BECAUSE I'M THE FIRST!
Pamila (Pam), Fellowship Manager
IT'S A BUSY-NESS CARD. IN CASE YOU'RE BUSY AND FORGET MY NAME.
I APPRECIATE YOUR DESIRE TO HELP.
BUT I ASSURE YOU, THERE IS NO NEED FOR YOU TO JOIN ME ON THIS QUEST.
BUT--

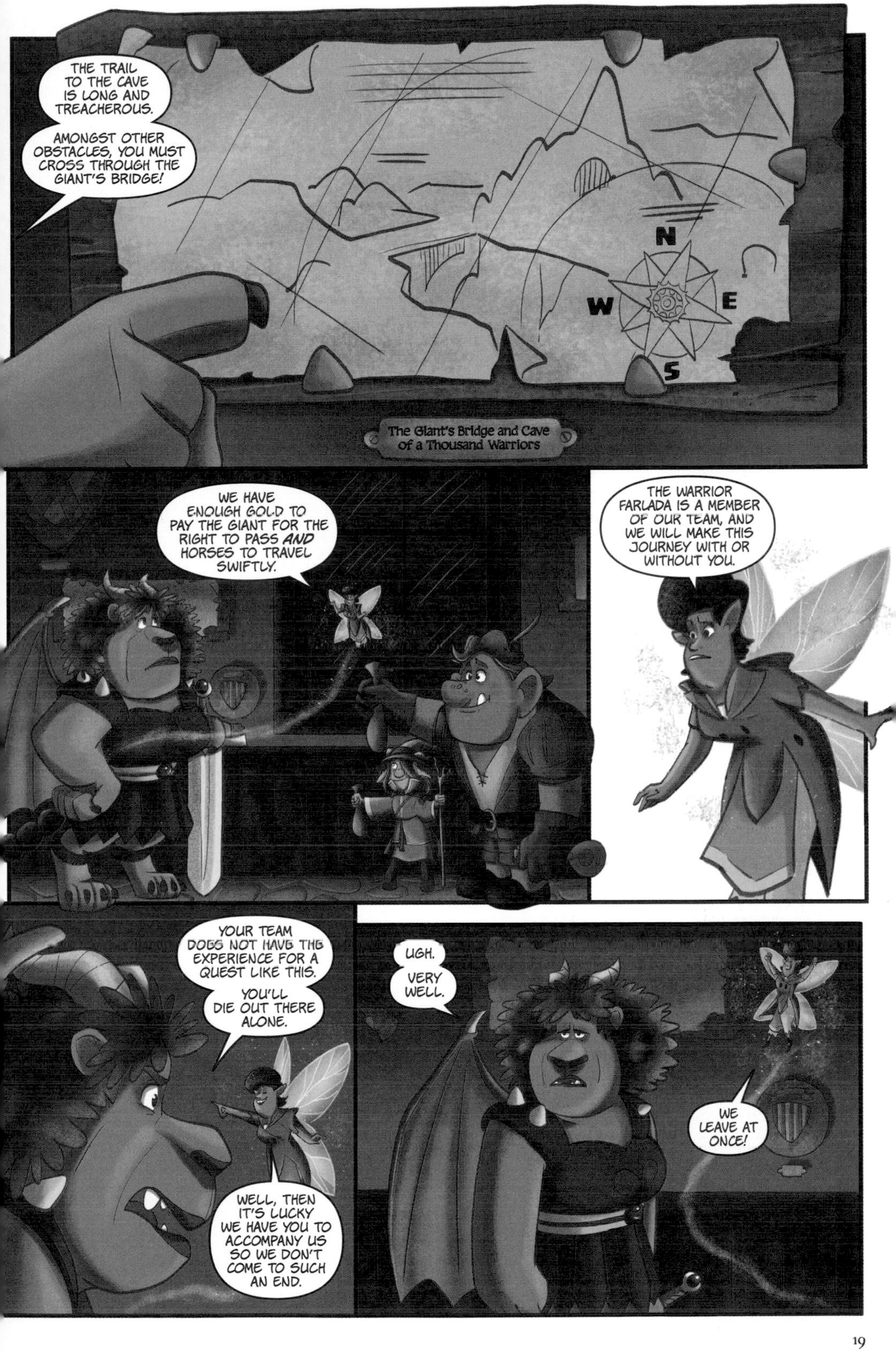
THE TRAIL TO THE CAVE IS LONG AND TREACHEROUS.
AMONGST OTHER OBSTACLES, YOU MUST CROSS THROUGH THE GIANT'S BRIDGE!
N
W
E
S
The Giant's Bridge and Cave of a Thousand Warriors
WE HAVE ENOUGH GOLD TO PAY THE GIANT FOR THE RIGHT TO PASS *AND* HORSES TO TRAVEL SWIFTLY.
THE WARRIOR FARLADA IS A MEMBER OF OUR TEAM, AND WE WILL MAKE THIS JOURNEY WITH OR WITHOUT YOU.
YOUR TEAM DOES NOT HAVE THE EXPERIENCE FOR A QUEST LIKE THIS.
YOU'LL DIE OUT THERE ALONE.
WELL, THEN IT'S LUCKY WE HAVE YOU TO ACCOMPANY US SO WE DON'T COME TO SUCH AN END.
UGH.
VERY WELL.
WE LEAVE AT ONCE!

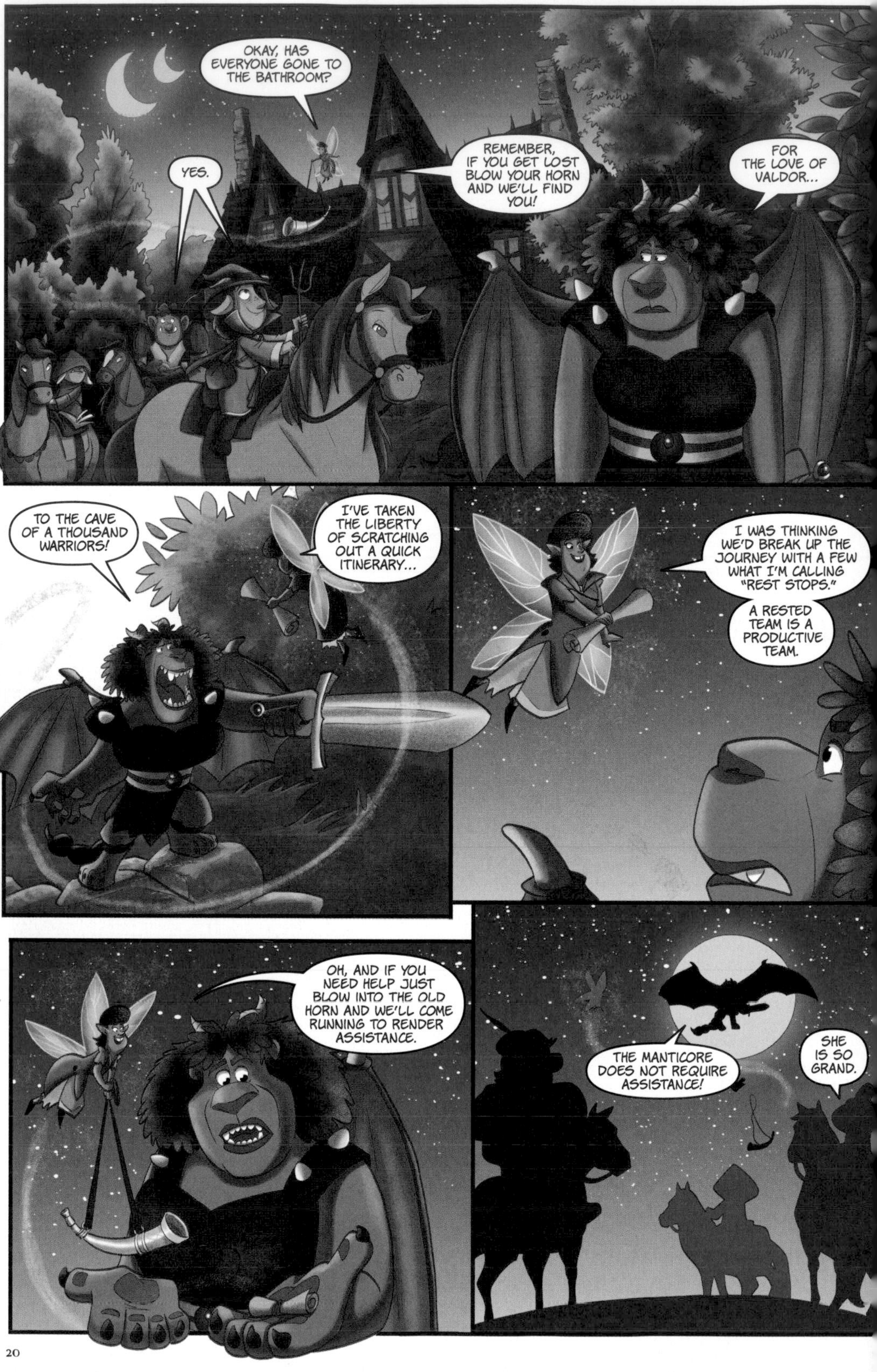
OKAY, HAS EVERYONE GONE TO THE BATHROOM?
YES.
REMEMBER, IF YOU GET LOST BLOW YOUR HORN AND WE'LL FIND YOU!
FOR THE LOVE OF VALDOR...
TO THE CAVE OF A THOUSAND WARRIORS!
I'VE TAKEN THE LIBERTY OF SCRATCHING OUT A QUICK ITINERARY...
I WAS THINKING WE'D BREAK UP THE JOURNEY WITH A FEW WHAT I'M CALLING "REST STOPS."
A RESTED TEAM IS A PRODUCTIVE TEAM.
OH, AND IF YOU NEED HELP JUST BLOW INTO THE OLD HORN AND WE'LL COME RUNNING TO RENDER ASSISTANCE.
THE MANTICORE DOES NOT REQUIRE ASSISTANCE!
SHE IS SO GRAND.

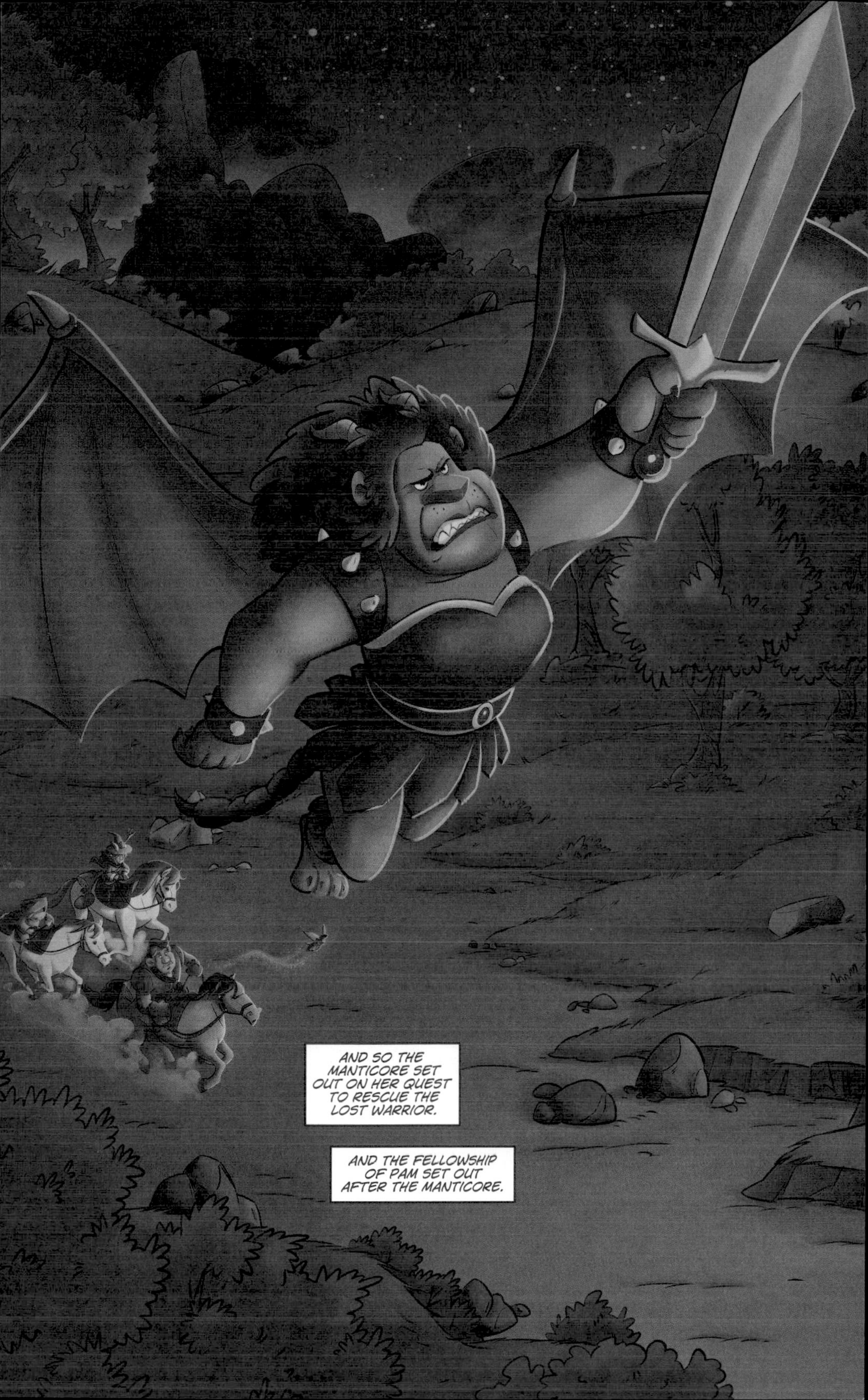
AND SO THE MANTICORE SET OUT ON HER QUEST TO RESCUE THE LOST WARRIOR.
AND THE FELLOWSHIP OF PAM SET OUT AFTER THE MANTICORE.

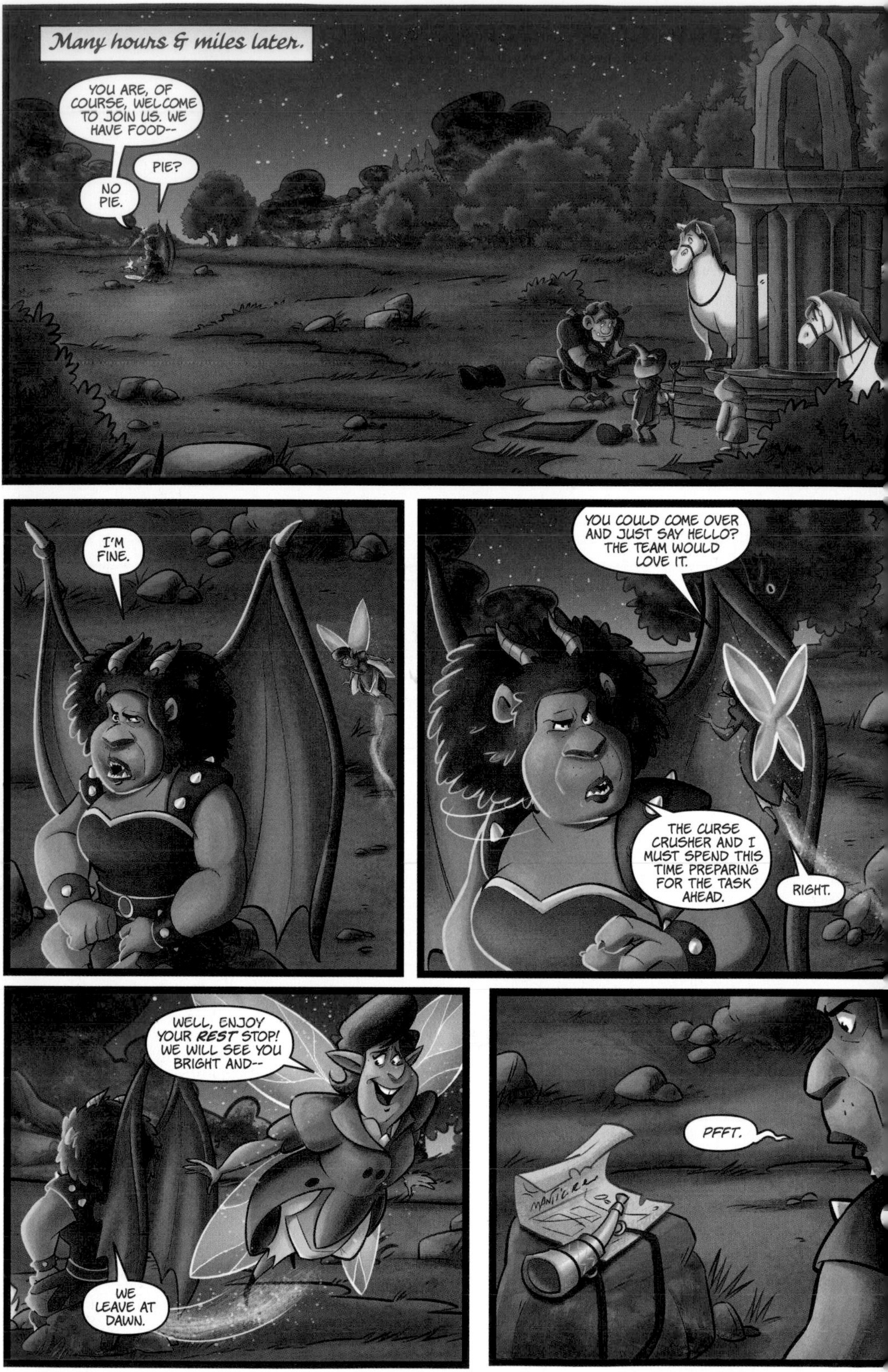
Many hours & miles later.
YOU ARE, OF COURSE, WELCOME TO JOIN US. WE HAVE FOOD--
PIE?
NO PIE.
I'M FINE.
YOU COULD COME OVER AND JUST SAY HELLO? THE TEAM WOULD LOVE IT.
THE CURSE CRUSHER AND I MUST SPEND THIS TIME PREPARING FOR THE TASK AHEAD.
RIGHT.
WELL, ENJOY YOUR *REST* STOP! WE WILL SEE YOU BRIGHT AND--
WE LEAVE AT DAWN.
PFFT.

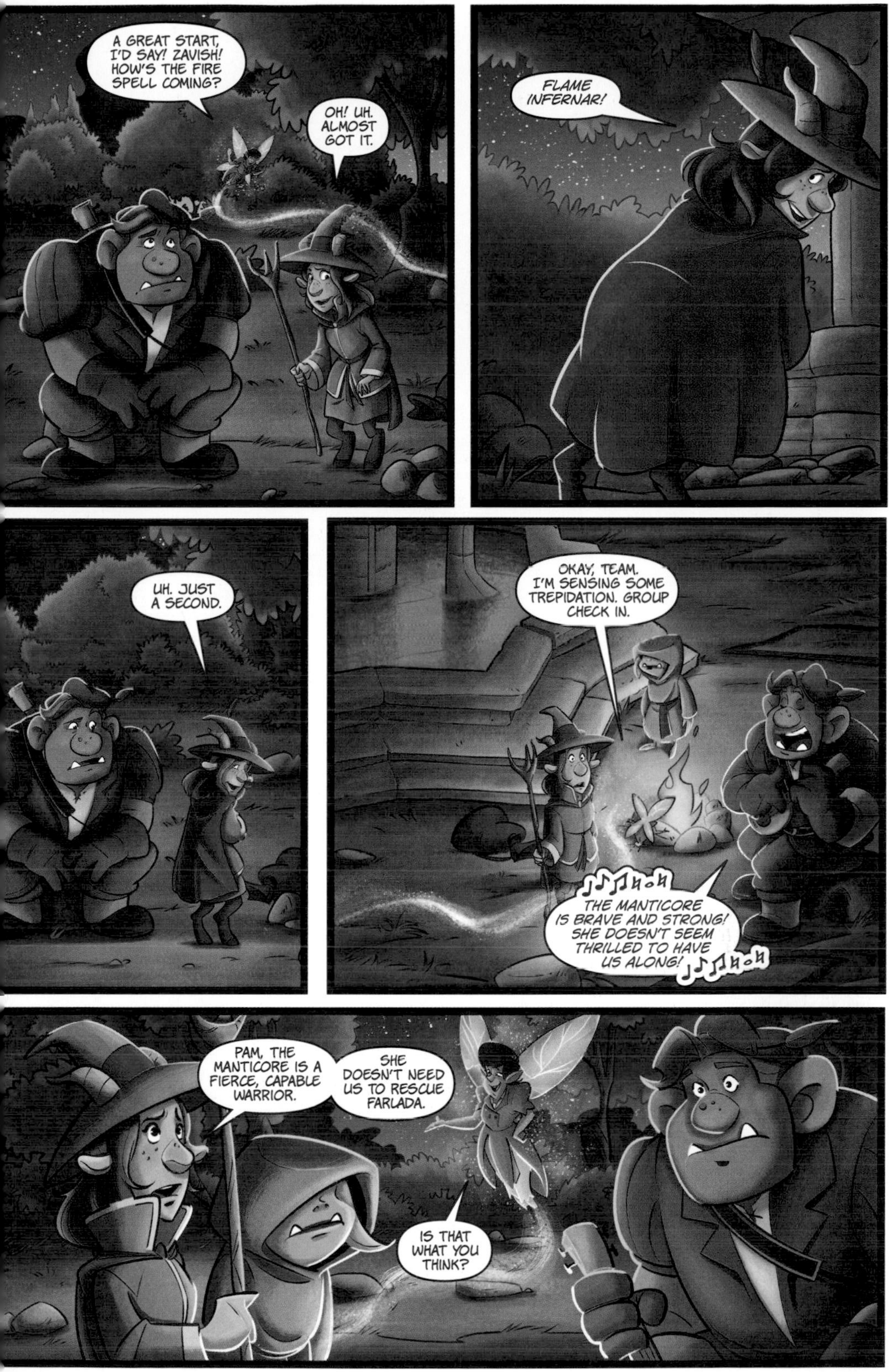
A GREAT START, I'D SAY! ZAVISH! HOW'S THE FIRE SPELL COMING?
OH! UH. ALMOST GOT IT.
FLAME INFERNAR!
UH. JUST A SECOND.
OKAY, TEAM. I'M SENSING SOME TREPIDATION. GROUP CHECK IN.
THE MANTICORE IS BRAVE AND STRONG! SHE DOESN'T SEEM THRILLED TO HAVE US ALONG!
PAM, THE MANTICORE IS A FIERCE, CAPABLE WARRIOR.
SHE DOESN'T NEED US TO RESCUE FARLADA.
IS THAT WHAT YOU THINK?

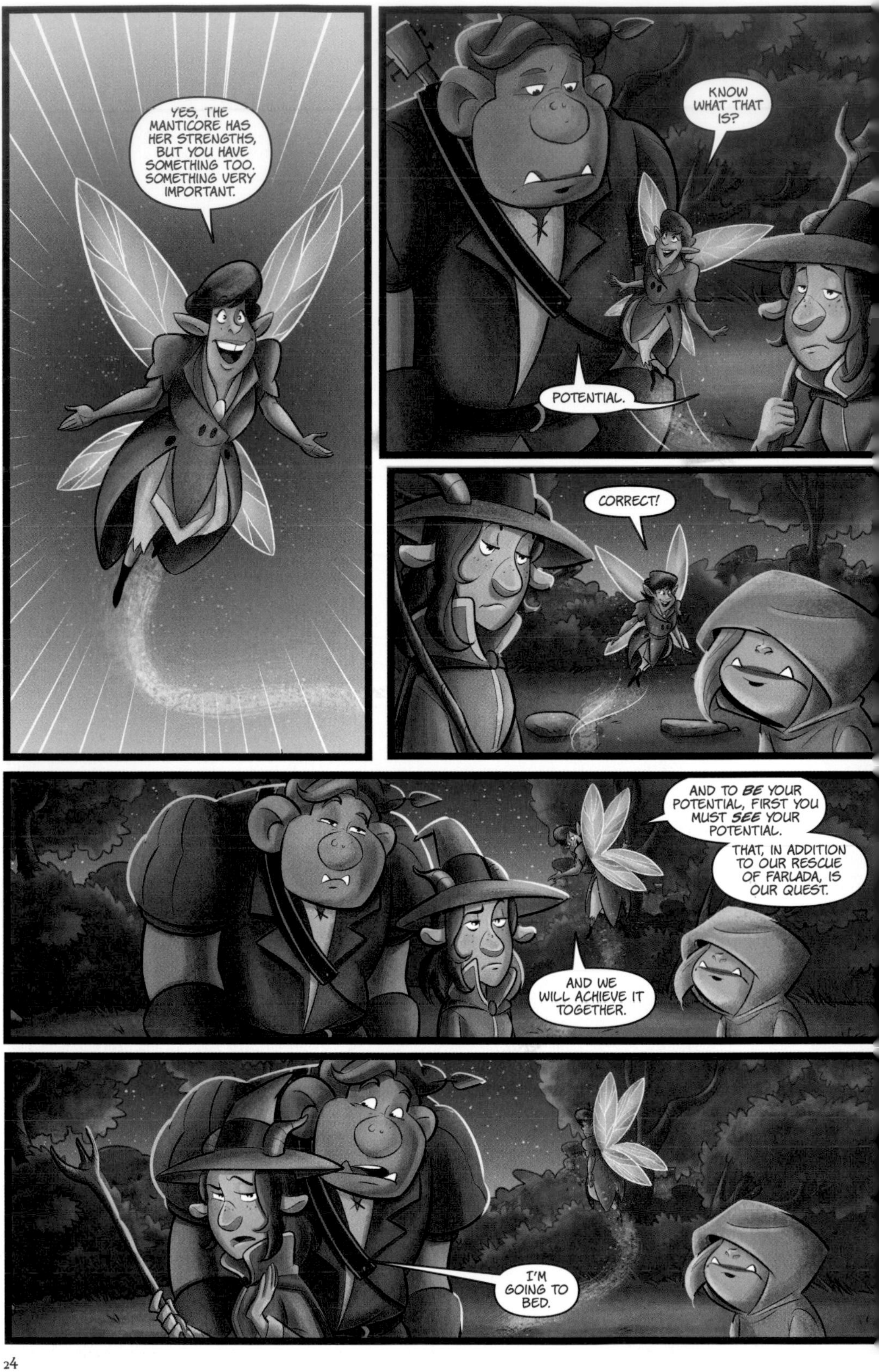
YES, THE MANTICORE HAS HER STRENGTHS, BUT YOU HAVE SOMETHING TOO. SOMETHING VERY IMPORTANT.
KNOW WHAT THAT IS?
POTENTIAL.
CORRECT!
AND TO BE YOUR POTENTIAL, FIRST YOU MUST SEE YOUR POTENTIAL.
THAT, IN ADDITION TO OUR RESCUE OF FARLADA, IS OUR QUEST.
AND WE WILL ACHIEVE IT TOGETHER.
I'M GOING TO BED.

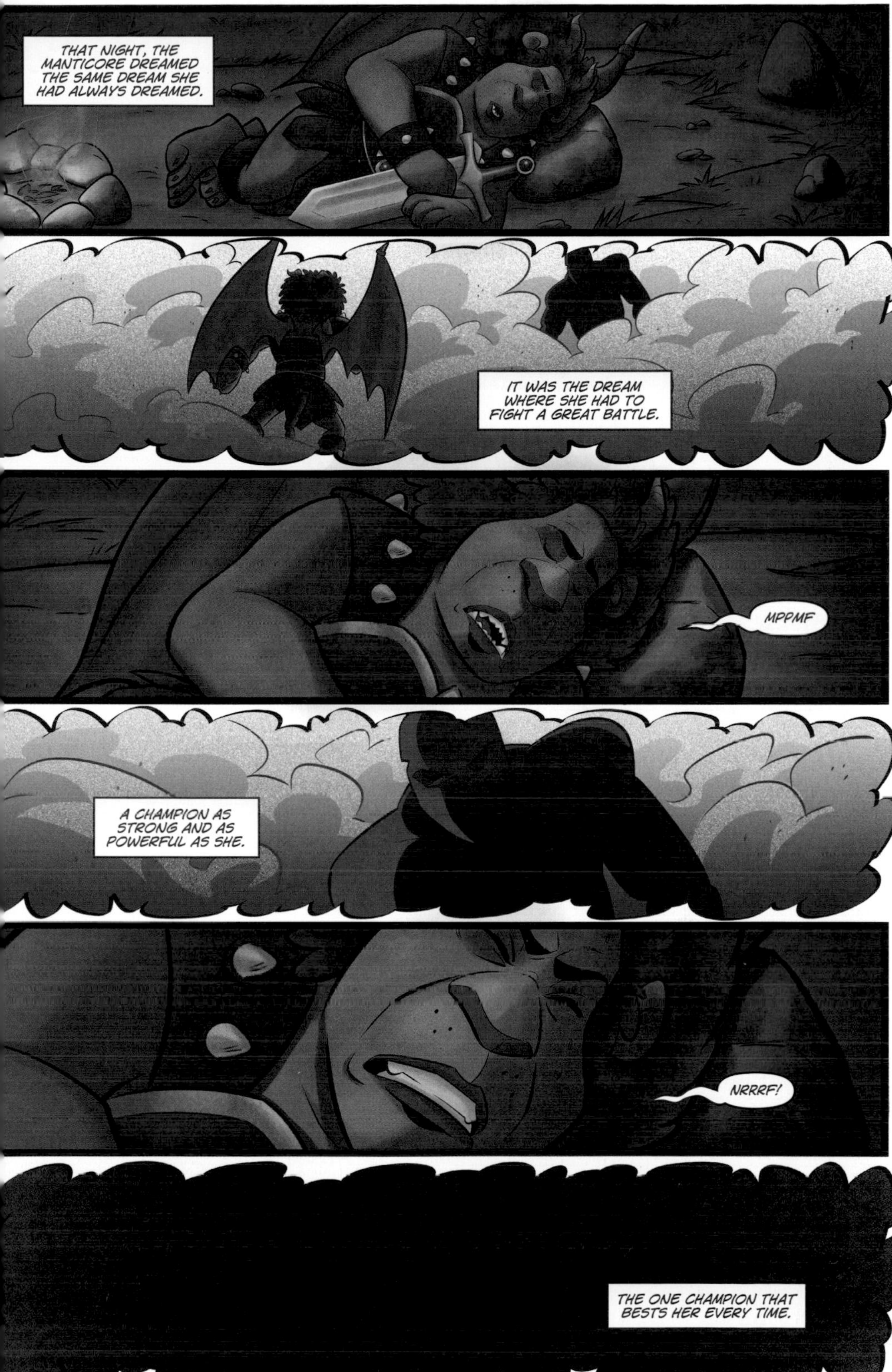
THAT NIGHT, THE MANTICORE DREAMED THE SAME DREAM SHE HAD ALWAYS DREAMED.
IT WAS THE DREAM WHERE SHE HAD TO FIGHT A GREAT BATTLE.
MPPMF
A CHAMPION AS STRONG AND AS POWERFUL AS SHE.
NRRRF!
THE ONE CHAMPION THAT BESTS HER EVERY TIME.

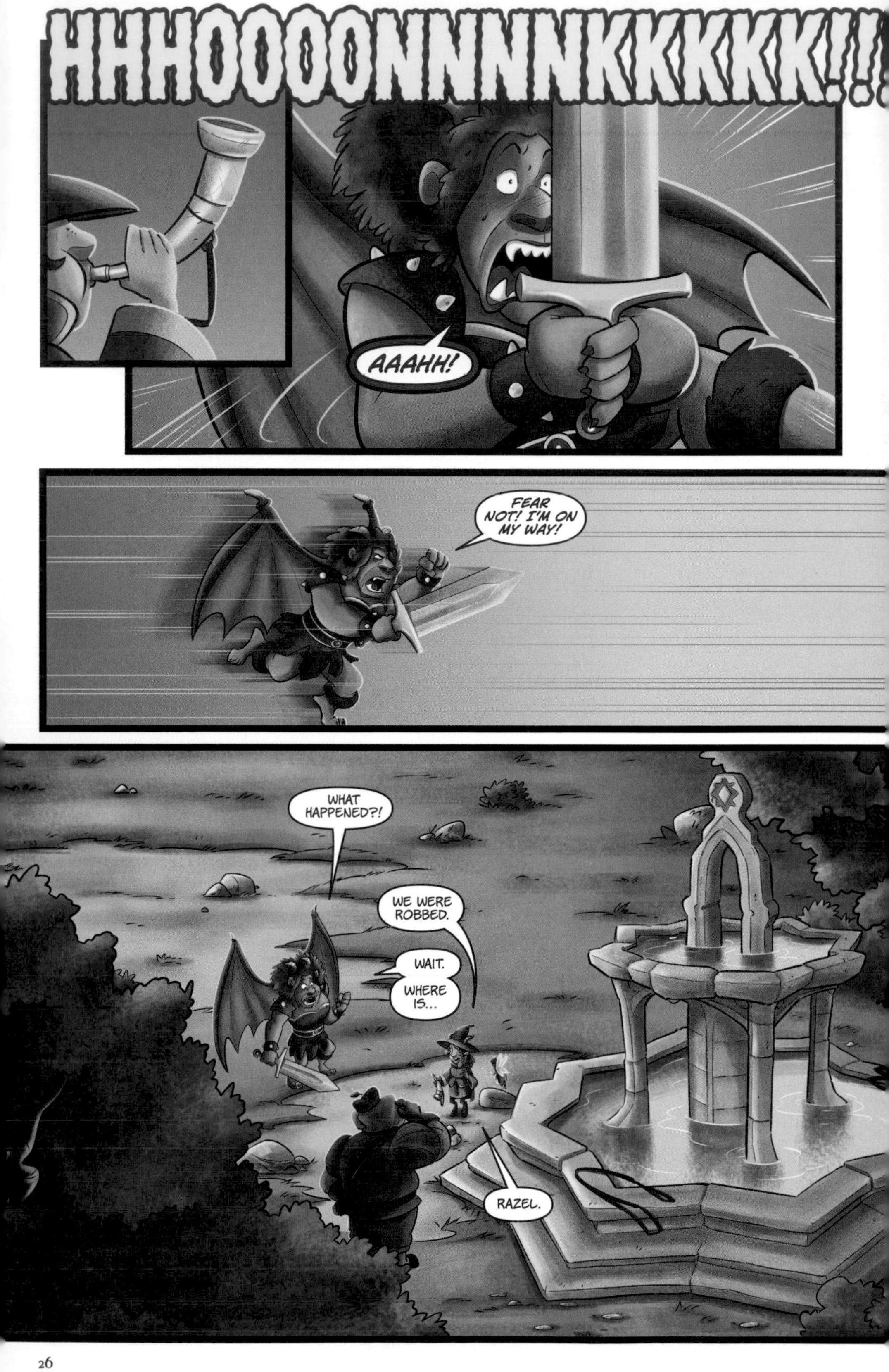
HHHOOOONNNNNKKKKKK!!!
AAAHH!
FEAR NOT! I'M ON MY WAY!
WHAT HAPPENED?!
WE WERE ROBBED.
WAIT.
WHERE IS...
RAZEL.

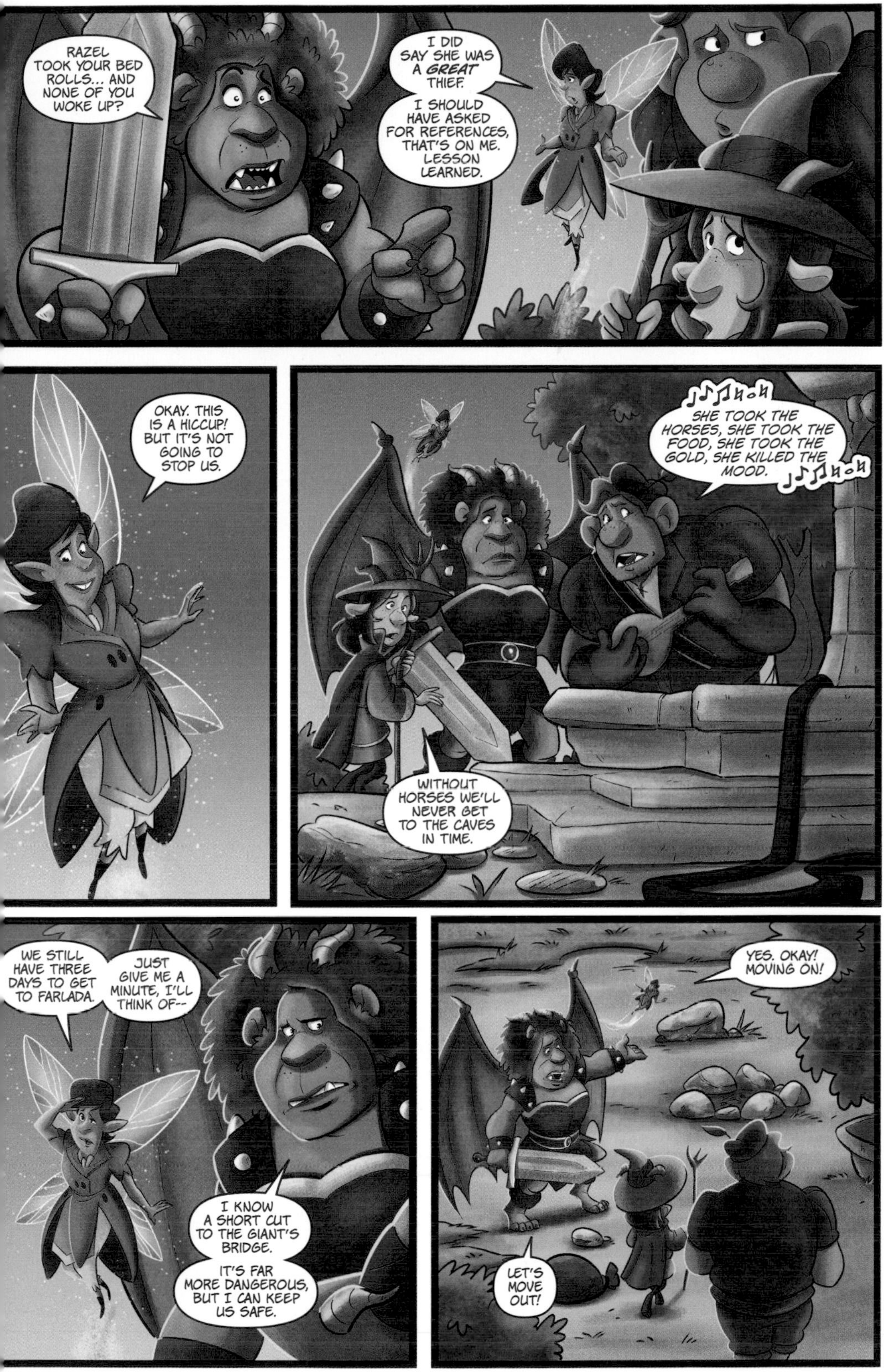
RAZEL TOOK YOUR BED ROLLS... AND NONE OF YOU WOKE UP?
I DID SAY SHE WAS A *GREAT* THIEF.
I SHOULD HAVE ASKED FOR REFERENCES, THAT'S ON ME. LESSON LEARNED.
OKAY. THIS IS A HICCUP! BUT IT'S NOT GOING TO STOP US.
SHE TOOK THE HORSES, SHE TOOK THE FOOD, SHE TOOK THE GOLD, SHE KILLED THE MOOD.
WITHOUT HORSES WE'LL NEVER GET TO THE CAVES IN TIME.
WE STILL HAVE THREE DAYS TO GET TO FARLADA.
JUST GIVE ME A MINUTE, I'LL THINK OF--
I KNOW A SHORT CUT TO THE GIANT'S BRIDGE.
IT'S FAR MORE DANGEROUS, BUT I CAN KEEP US SAFE.
YES. OKAY! MOVING ON!
LET'S MOVE OUT!

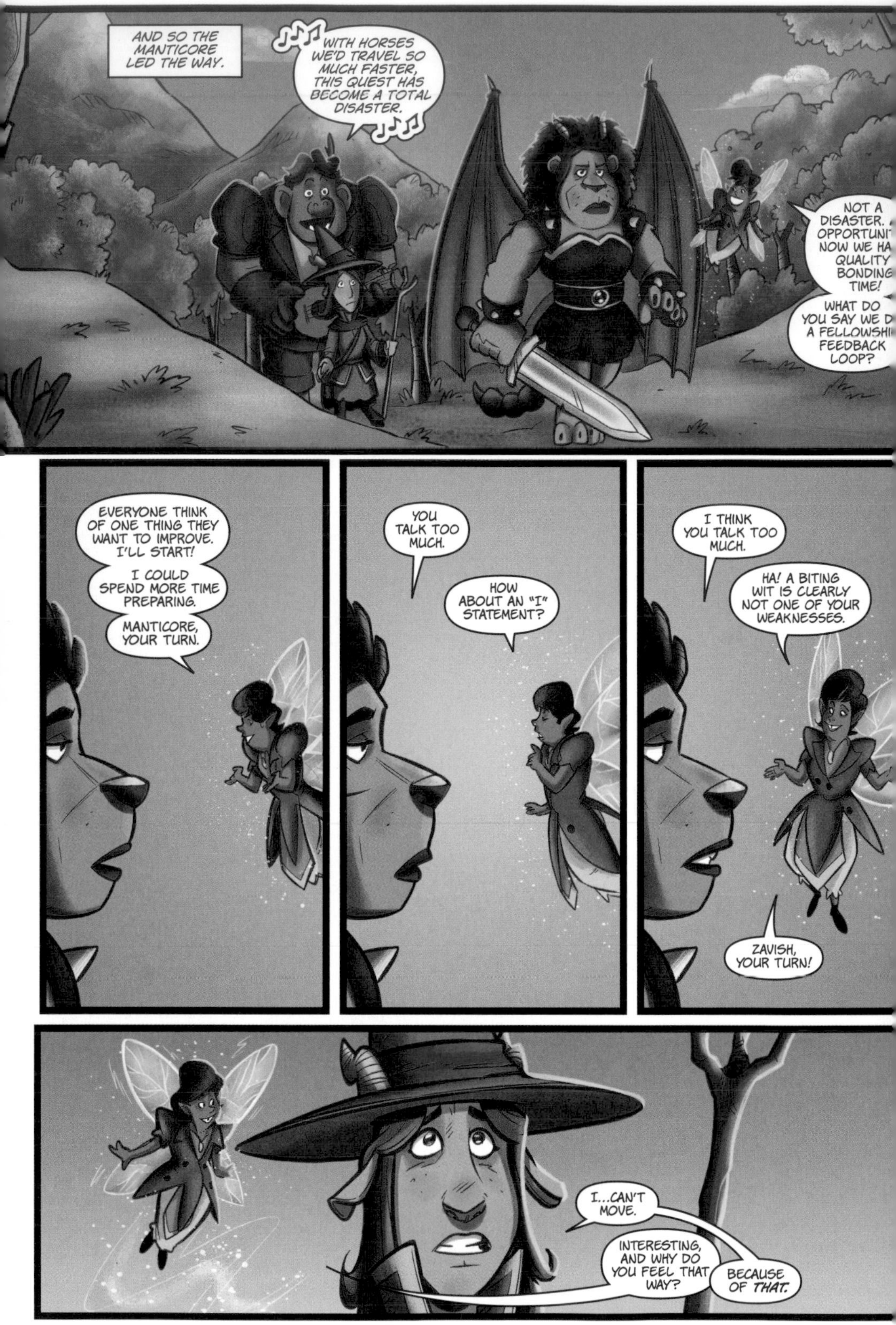
AND SO THE MANTICORE LED THE WAY.
WITH HORSES WE'D TRAVEL SO MUCH FASTER, THIS QUEST HAS BECOME A TOTAL DISASTER.
NOT A DISASTER. OPPORTUNI NOW WE HA QUALITY BONDING TIME!
WHAT DO YOU SAY WE D A FELLOWSHI FEEDBACK LOOP?
EVERYONE THINK OF ONE THING THEY WANT TO IMPROVE. I'LL START!
I COULD SPEND MORE TIME PREPARING.
MANTICORE, YOUR TURN.
YOU TALK TOO MUCH.
HOW ABOUT AN "I" STATEMENT?
I THINK YOU TALK TOO MUCH.
HA! A BITING WIT IS CLEARLY NOT ONE OF YOUR WEAKNESSES.
ZAVISH, YOUR TURN!
I...CAN'T MOVE.
INTERESTING, AND WHY DO YOU FEEL THAT WAY?
BECAUSE OF THAT.

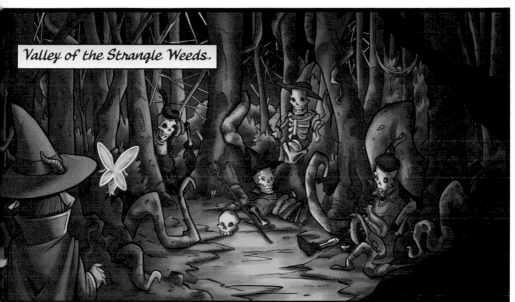

Valley of the Strangle Weeds.

OKAY. OUR NEXT CHALLENGE! YES!

ZAVISH, PREPARE YOUR FREEZING SPELL.

HORG, A ROUSING SCORE TO LIFT OUR SPIRITS.

MANTICORE--

AHHHHH!!!

UH, MANTICORE?

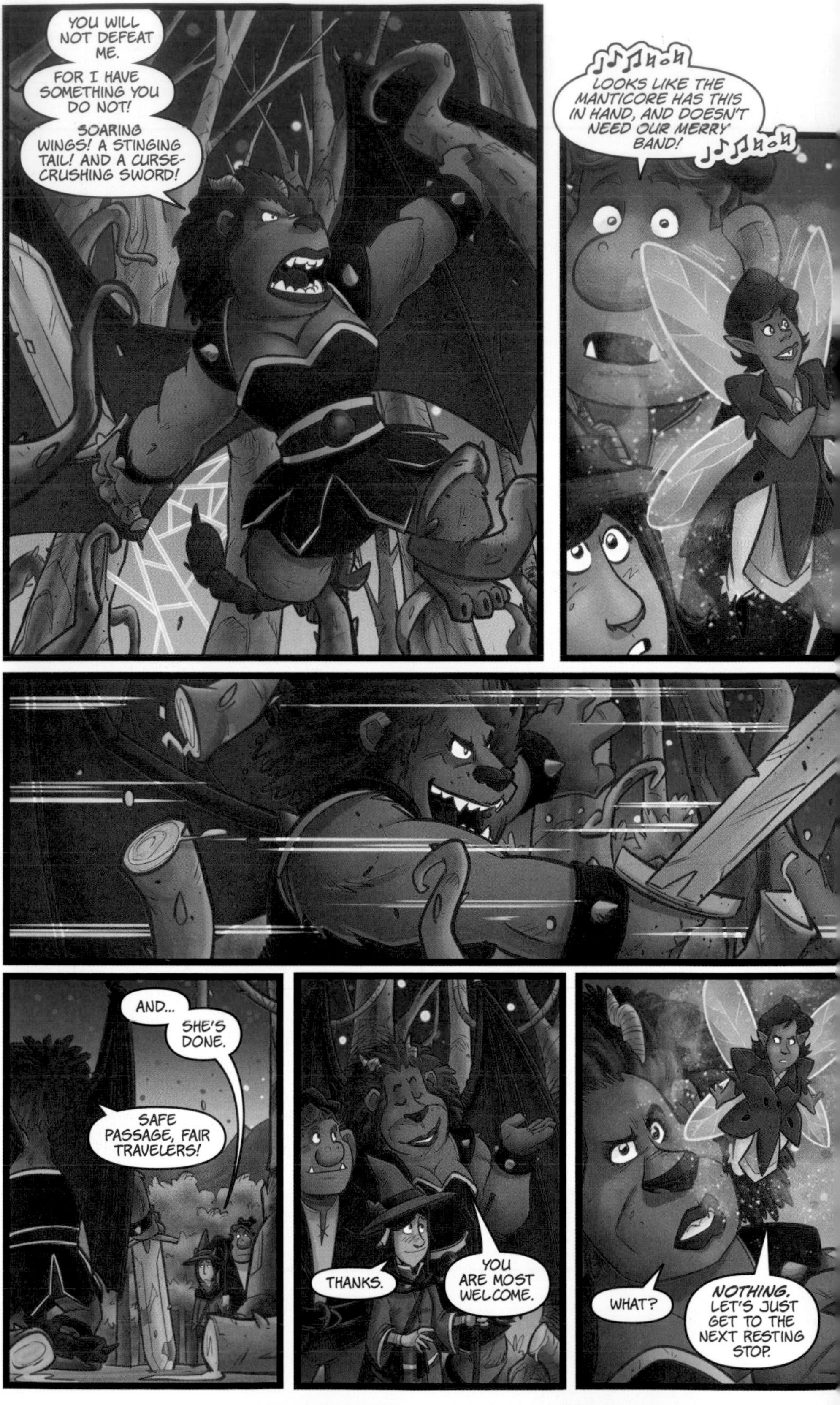
YOU WILL NOT DEFEAT ME.
FOR I HAVE SOMETHING YOU DO NOT!
SOARING WINGS! A STINGING TAIL! AND A CURSE-CRUSHING SWORD!
LOOKS LIKE THE MANTICORE HAS THIS IN HAND, AND DOESN'T NEED OUR MERRY BAND!
AND...
SHE'S DONE.
SAFE PASSAGE, FAIR TRAVELERS!
THANKS.
YOU ARE MOST WELCOME.
WHAT?
NOTHING. LET'S JUST GET TO THE NEXT RESTING STOP.

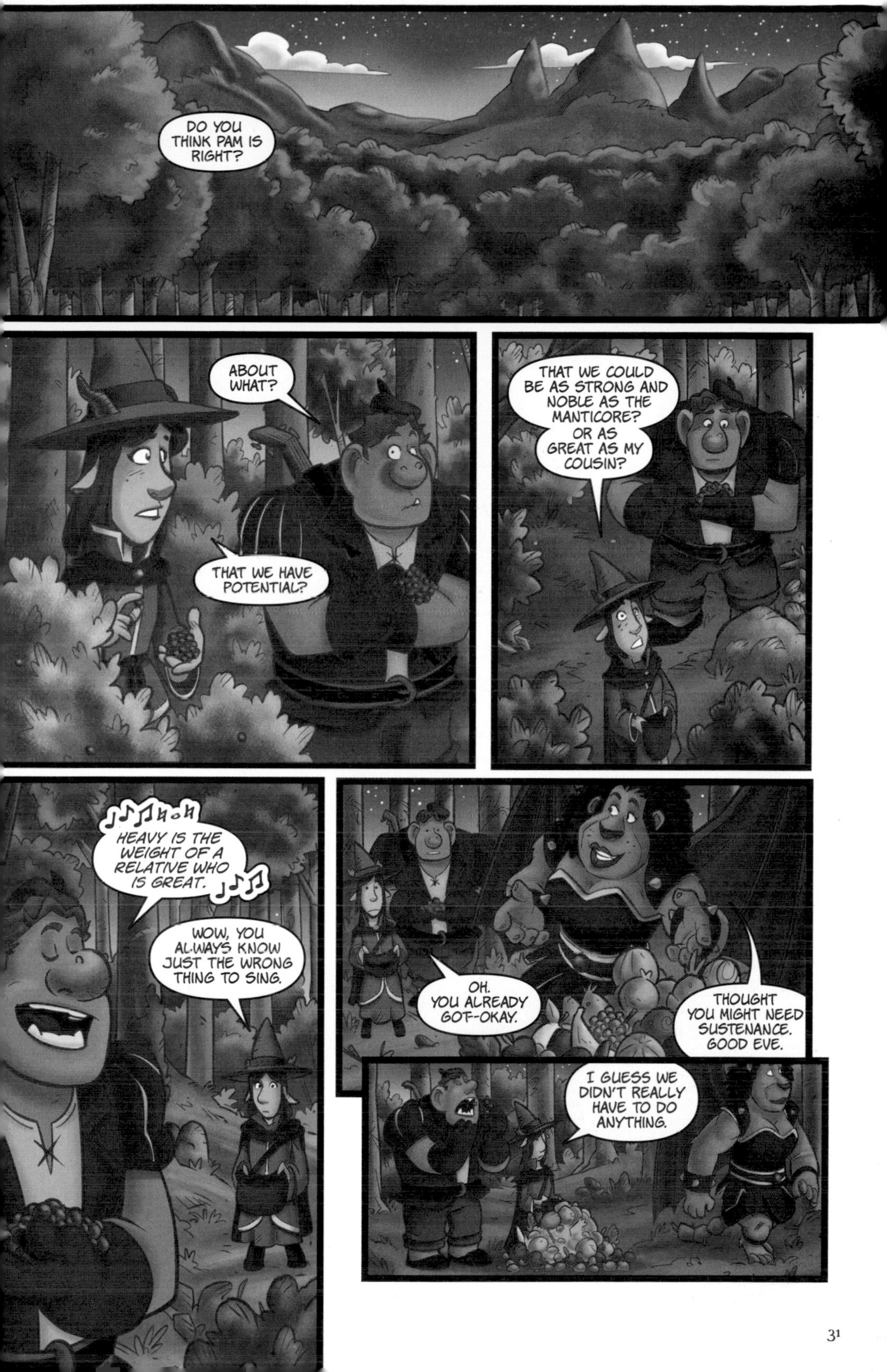
DO YOU THINK PAM IS RIGHT?
ABOUT WHAT?
THAT WE HAVE POTENTIAL?
THAT WE COULD BE AS STRONG AND NOBLE AS THE MANTICORE? OR AS GREAT AS MY COUSIN?
HEAVY IS THE WEIGHT OF A RELATIVE WHO IS GREAT.
WOW, YOU AL-WAYS KNOW JUST THE WRONG THING TO SING.
OH. YOU ALREADY GOT--OKAY.
THOUGHT YOU MIGHT NEED SUSTENANCE. GOOD EVE.
I GUESS WE DIDN'T REALLY HAVE TO DO ANYTHING.

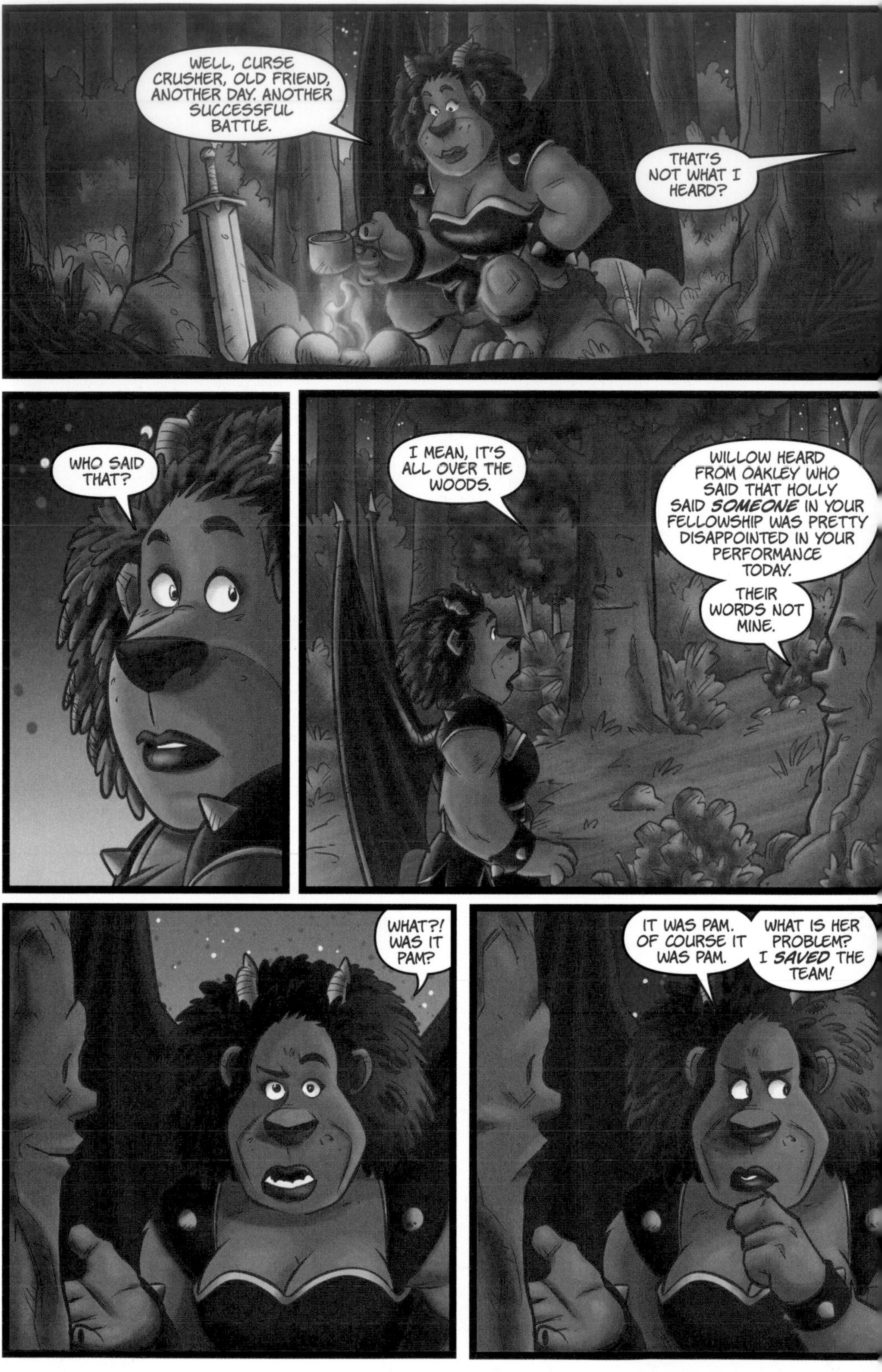
WELL, CURSE CRUSHER, OLD FRIEND, ANOTHER DAY. ANOTHER SUCCESSFUL BATTLE.
THAT'S NOT WHAT I HEARD?
WHO SAID THAT?
I MEAN, IT'S ALL OVER THE WOODS.
WILLOW HEARD FROM OAKLEY WHO SAID THAT HOLLY SAID SOMEONE IN YOUR FELLOWSHIP WAS PRETTY DISAPPOINTED IN YOUR PERFORMANCE TODAY.
THEIR WORDS NOT MINE.
WHAT?! WAS IT PAM?
IT WAS PAM. OF COURSE IT WAS PAM.
WHAT IS HER PROBLEM? I SAVED THE TEAM!

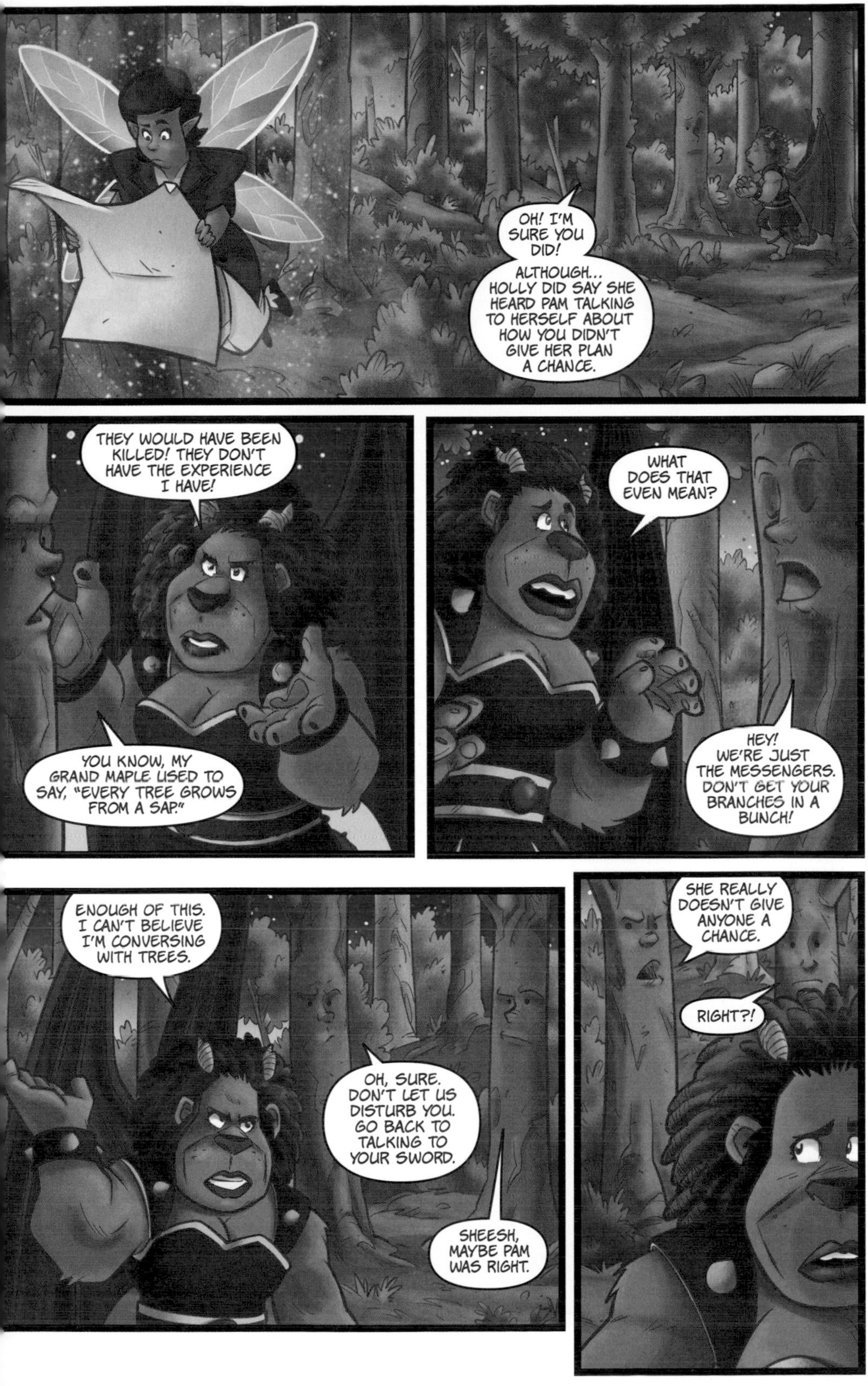
OH! I'M SURE YOU DID!
ALTHOUGH... HOLLY DID SAY SHE HEARD PAM TALKING TO HERSELF ABOUT HOW YOU DIDN'T GIVE HER PLAN A CHANCE.
THEY WOULD HAVE BEEN KILLED! THEY DON'T HAVE THE EXPERIENCE I HAVE!
YOU KNOW, MY GRAND MAPLE USED TO SAY, "EVERY TREE GROWS FROM A SAP."
WHAT DOES THAT EVEN MEAN?
HEY! WE'RE JUST THE MESSENGERS. DON'T GET YOUR BRANCHES IN A BUNCH!
ENOUGH OF THIS. I CAN'T BELIEVE I'M CONVERSING WITH TREES.
OH, SURE. DON'T LET US DISTURB YOU. GO BACK TO TALKING TO YOUR SWORD.
SHEESH, MAYBE PAM WAS RIGHT.
SHE REALLY DOESN'T GIVE ANYONE A CHANCE.
RIGHT?!

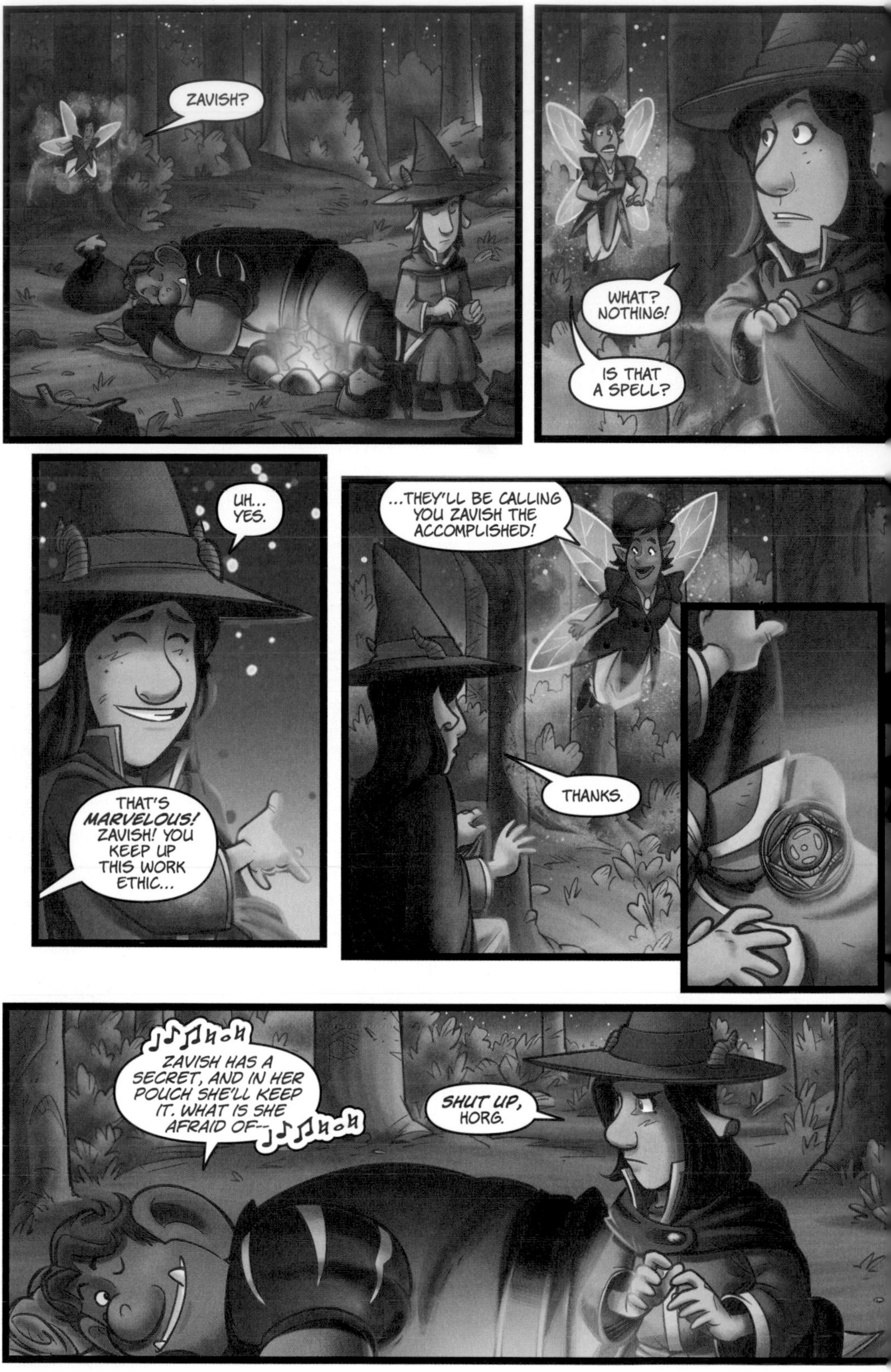
ZAVISH?
WHAT? NOTHING!
IS THAT A SPELL?
UH... YES.
THAT'S *MARVELOUS!* ZAVISH! YOU KEEP UP THIS WORK ETHIC...
...THEY'LL BE CALLING YOU ZAVISH THE ACCOMPLISHED!
THANKS.
ZAVISH HAS A SECRET, AND IN HER POUCH SHE'LL KEEP IT. WHAT IS SHE AFRAID OF--
SHUT UP, HORG.

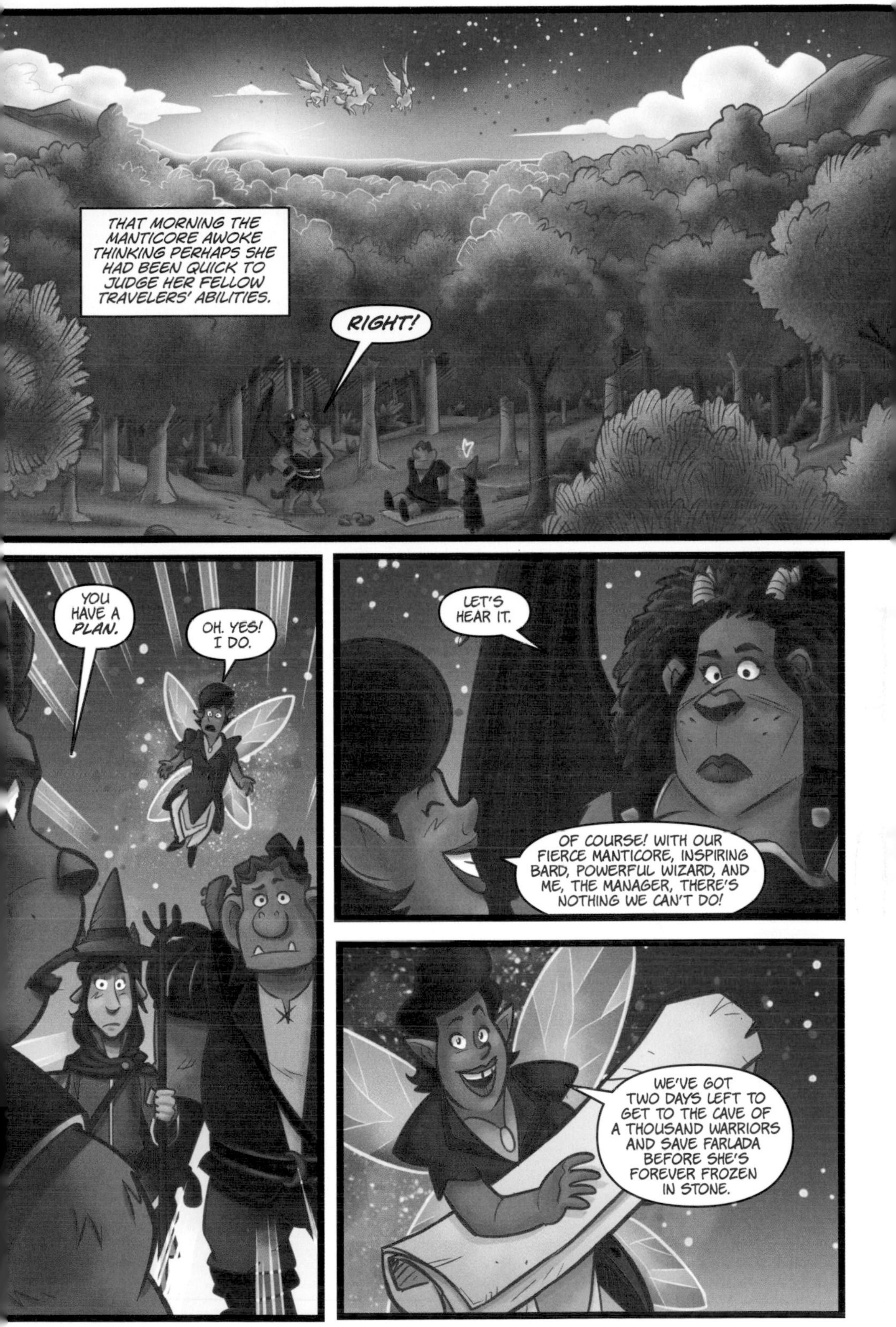
THAT MORNING THE MANTICORE AWOKE THINKING PERHAPS SHE HAD BEEN QUICK TO JUDGE HER FELLOW TRAVELERS' ABILITIES.
RIGHT!
YOU HAVE A PLAN.
OH. YES! I DO.
LET'S HEAR IT.
OF COURSE! WITH OUR FIERCE MANTICORE, INSPIRING BARD, POWERFUL WIZARD, AND ME, THE MANAGER, THERE'S NOTHING WE CAN'T DO!
WE'VE GOT TWO DAYS LEFT TO GET TO THE CAVE OF A THOUSAND WARRIORS AND SAVE FARLADA BEFORE SHE'S FOREVER FROZEN IN STONE.

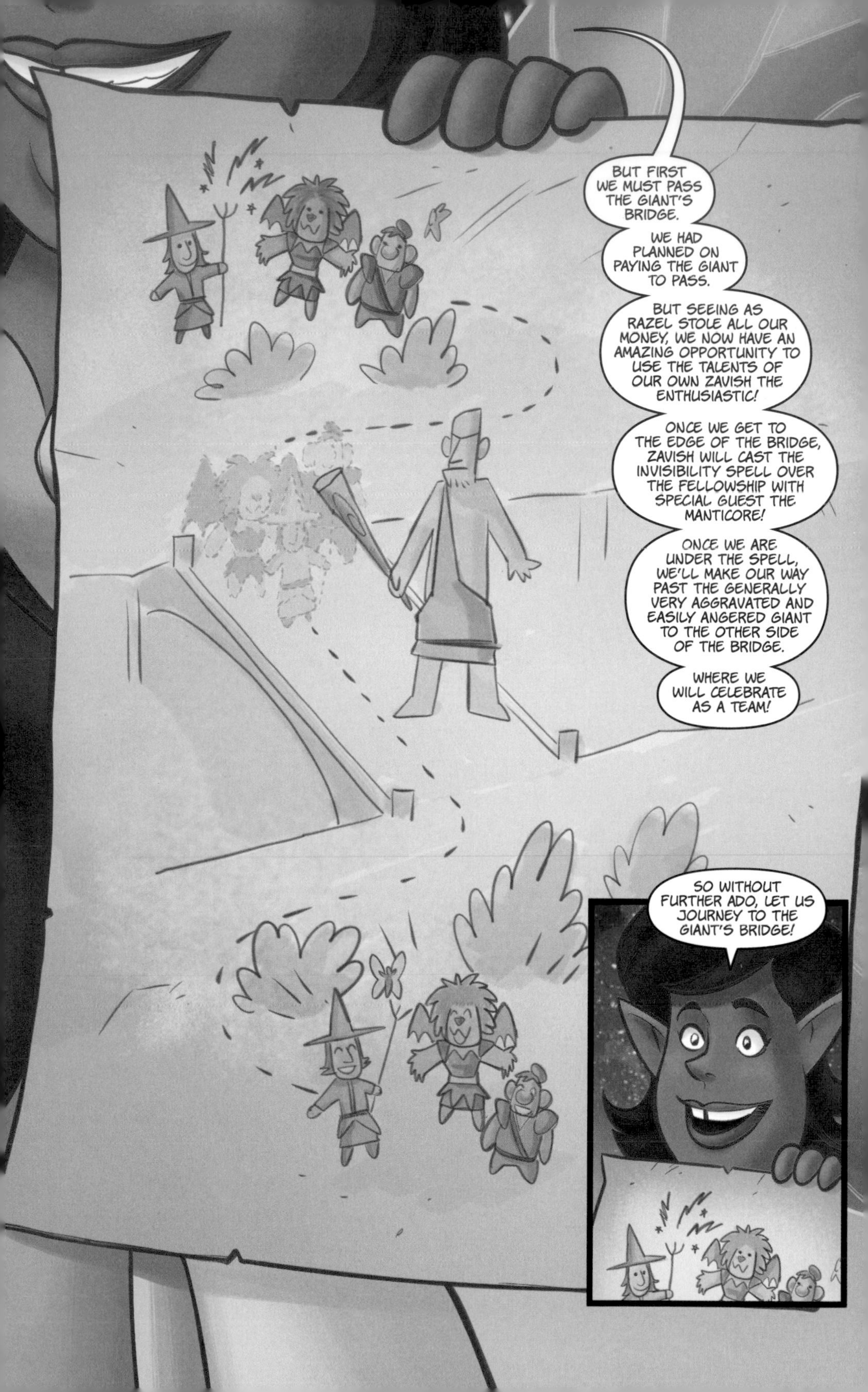
BUT FIRST WE MUST PASS THE GIANT'S BRIDGE.
WE HAD PLANNED ON PAYING THE GIANT TO PASS.
BUT SEEING AS RAZEL STOLE ALL OUR MONEY, WE NOW HAVE AN AMAZING OPPORTUNITY TO USE THE TALENTS OF OUR OWN ZAVISH THE ENTHUSIASTIC!
ONCE WE GET TO THE EDGE OF THE BRIDGE, ZAVISH WILL CAST THE INVISIBILITY SPELL OVER THE FELLOWSHIP WITH SPECIAL GUEST THE MANTICORE!
ONCE WE ARE UNDER THE SPELL, WE'LL MAKE OUR WAY PAST THE GENERALLY VERY AGGRAVATED AND EASILY ANGERED GIANT TO THE OTHER SIDE OF THE BRIDGE.
WHERE WE WILL CELEBRATE AS A TEAM!
SO WITHOUT FURTHER ADO, LET US JOURNEY TO THE GIANT'S BRIDGE!

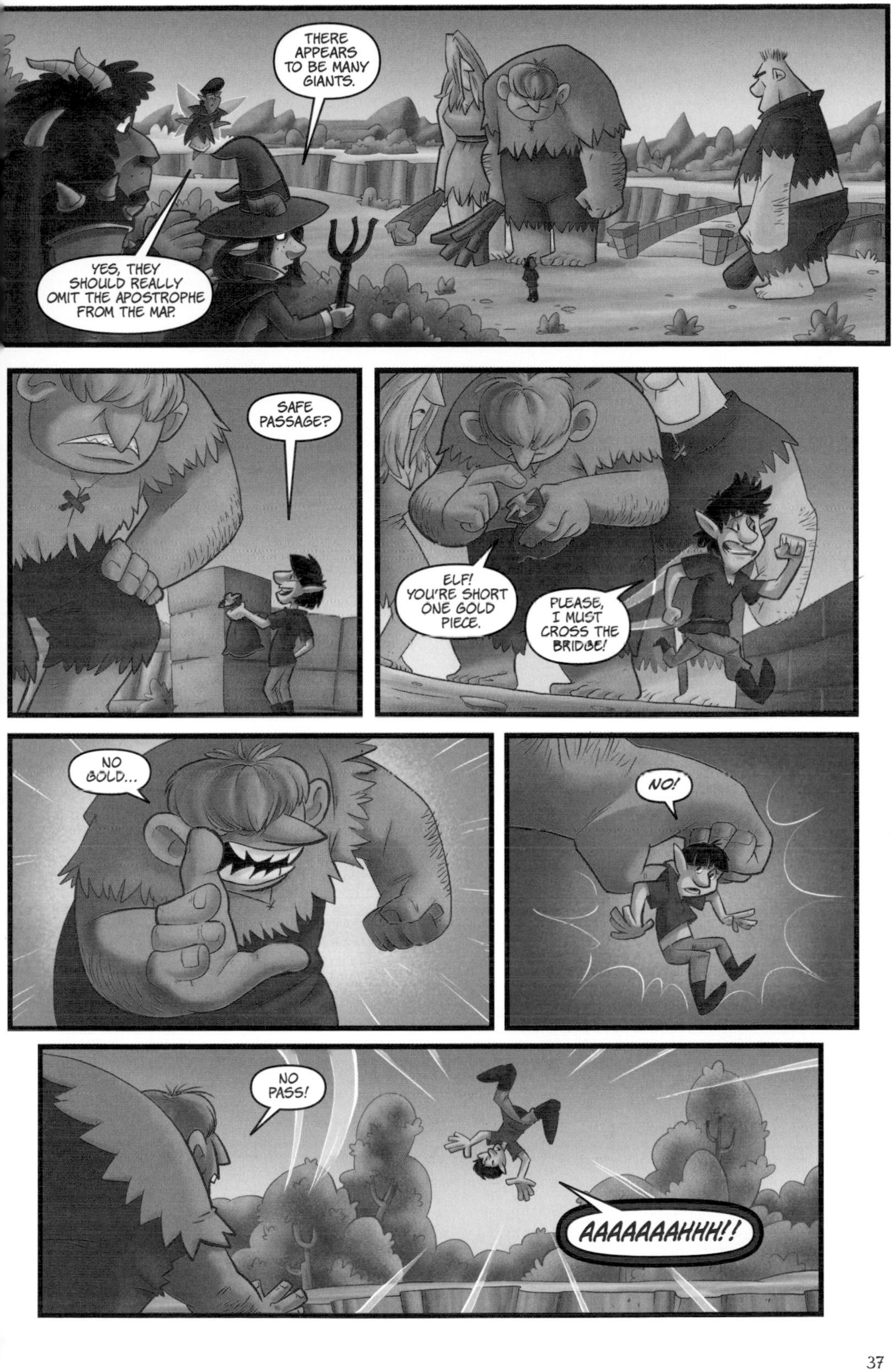
THERE APPEARS TO BE MANY GIANTS.
YES, THEY SHOULD REALLY OMIT THE APOSTROPHE FROM THE MAP.
SAFE PASSAGE?
ELF! YOU'RE SHORT ONE GOLD PIECE.
PLEASE, I MUST CROSS THE BRIDGE!
NO GOLD...
NO!
NO PASS!
AAAAAAAHHH!!

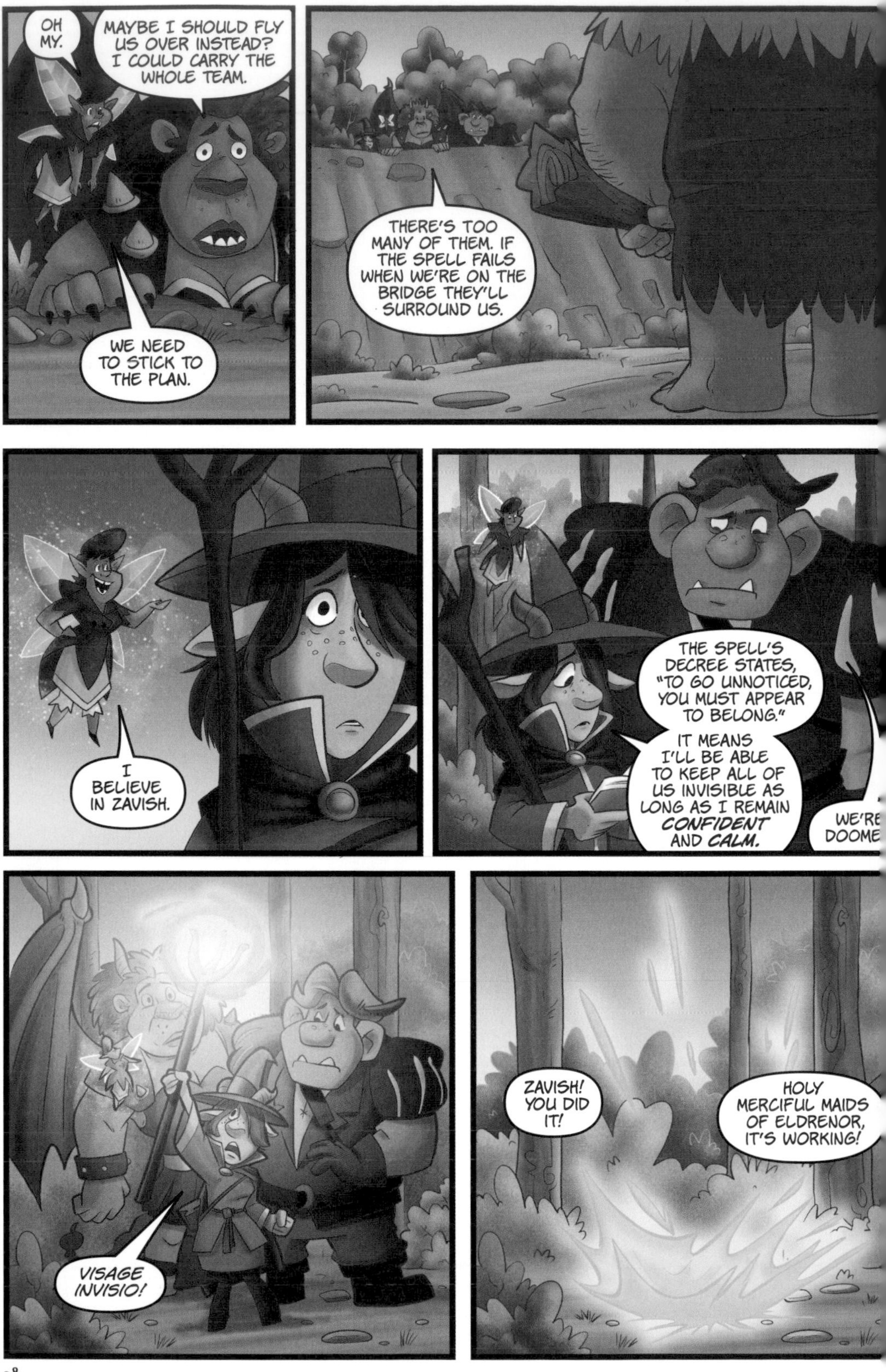
OH MY.
MAYBE I SHOULD FLY US OVER INSTEAD? I COULD CARRY THE WHOLE TEAM.
WE NEED TO STICK TO THE PLAN.
THERE'S TOO MANY OF THEM. IF THE SPELL FAILS WHEN WE'RE ON THE BRIDGE THEY'LL SURROUND US.
I BELIEVE IN ZAVISH.
THE SPELL'S DECREE STATES, "TO GO UNNOTICED, YOU MUST APPEAR TO BELONG."
IT MEANS I'LL BE ABLE TO KEEP ALL OF US INVISIBLE AS LONG AS I REMAIN ***CONFIDENT*** AND ***CALM.***
WE'RE DOOME
VISAGE INVISIO!
ZAVISH! YOU DID IT!
HOLY MERCIFUL MAIDS OF ELDRENOR, IT'S WORKING!

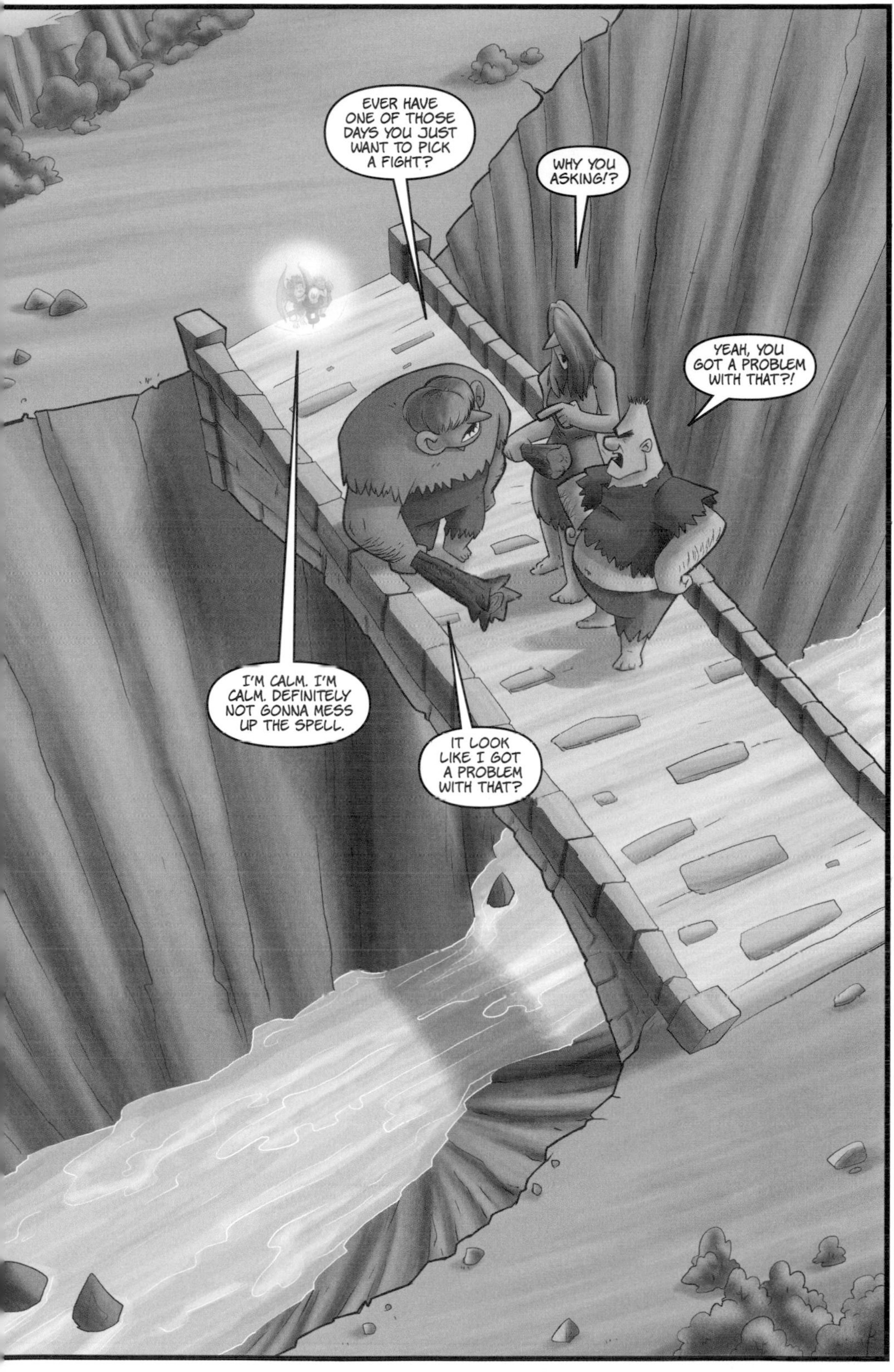
EVER HAVE ONE OF THOSE DAYS YOU JUST WANT TO PICK A FIGHT?
WHY YOU ASKING!?
YEAH, YOU GOT A PROBLEM WITH THAT?!
I'M CALM. I'M CALM. DEFINITELY NOT GONNA MESS UP THE SPELL.
IT LOOK LIKE I GOT A PROBLEM WITH THAT?

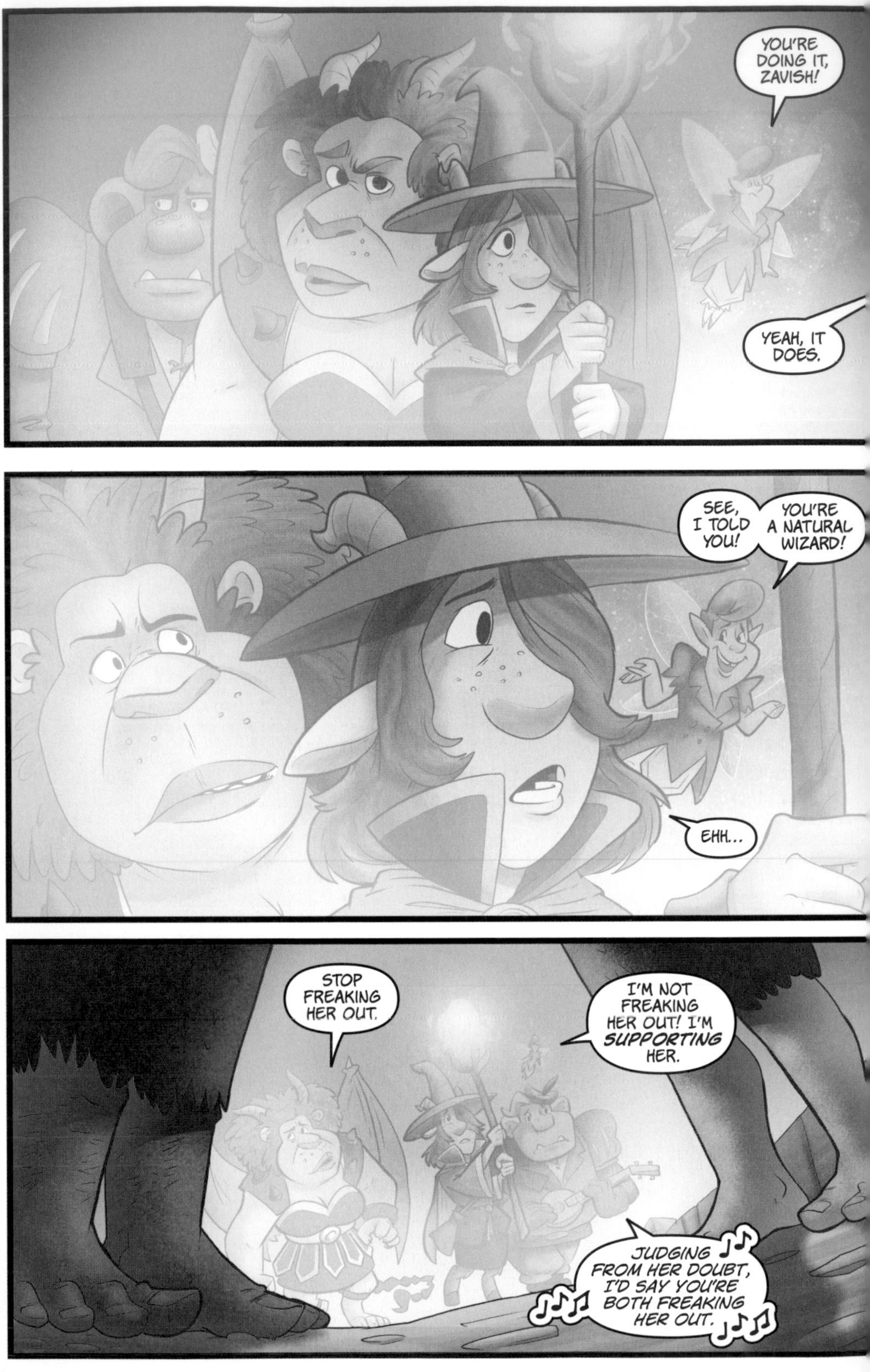
YOU'RE DOING IT, ZAVISH!
YEAH, IT DOES.
SEE, I TOLD YOU!
YOU'RE A NATURAL WIZARD!
EHH...
STOP FREAKING HER OUT.
I'M NOT FREAKING HER OUT! I'M SUPPORTING HER.
JUDGING FROM HER DOUBT, I'D SAY YOU'RE BOTH FREAKING HER OUT.

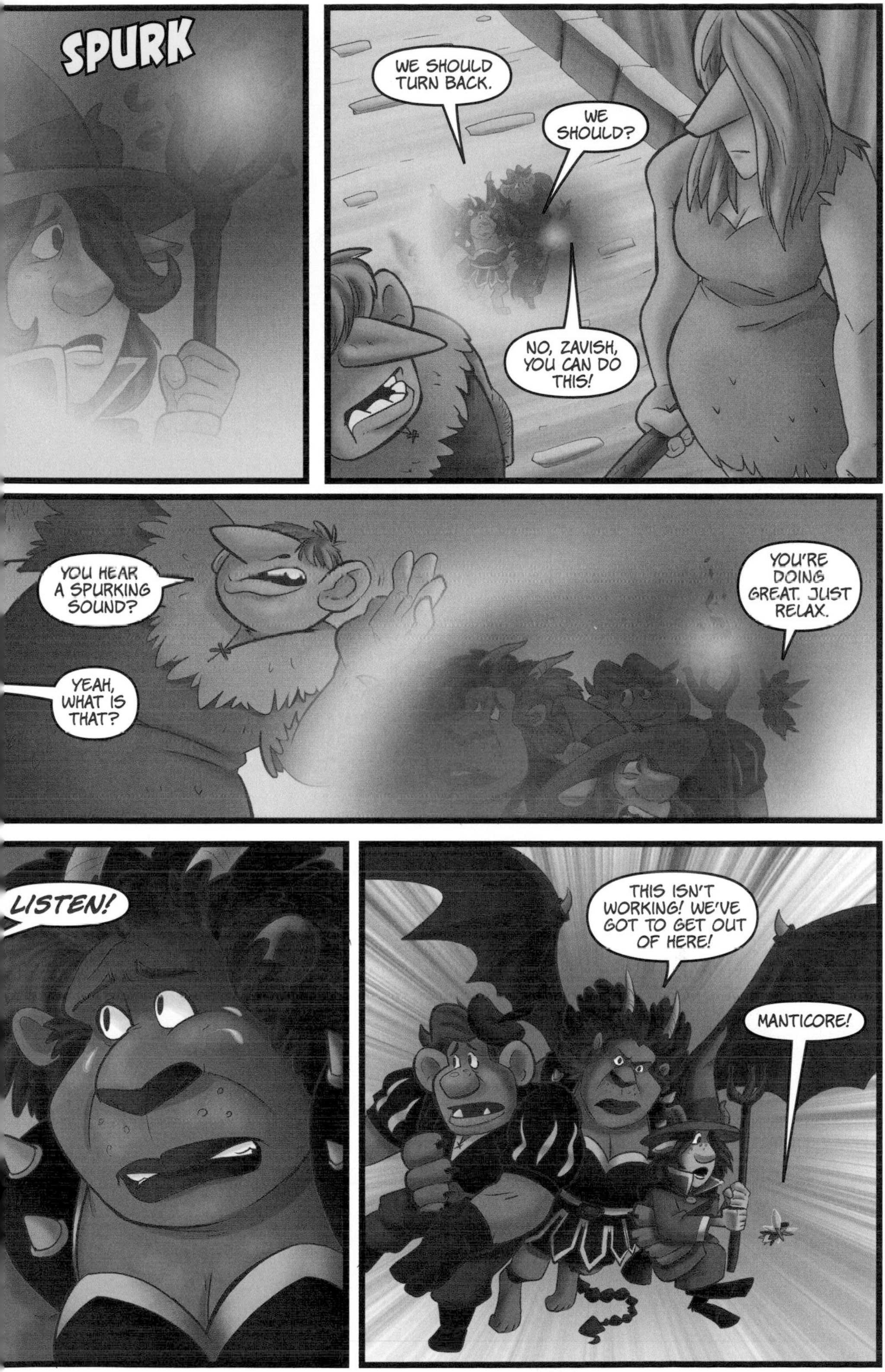
SPURK
WE SHOULD TURN BACK.
WE SHOULD?
NO, ZAVISH, YOU CAN DO THIS!
YOU HEAR A SPURKING SOUND?
YEAH, WHAT IS THAT?
YOU'RE DOING GREAT. JUST RELAX.
LISTEN!
THIS ISN'T WORKING! WE'VE GOT TO GET OUT OF HERE!
MANTICORE!

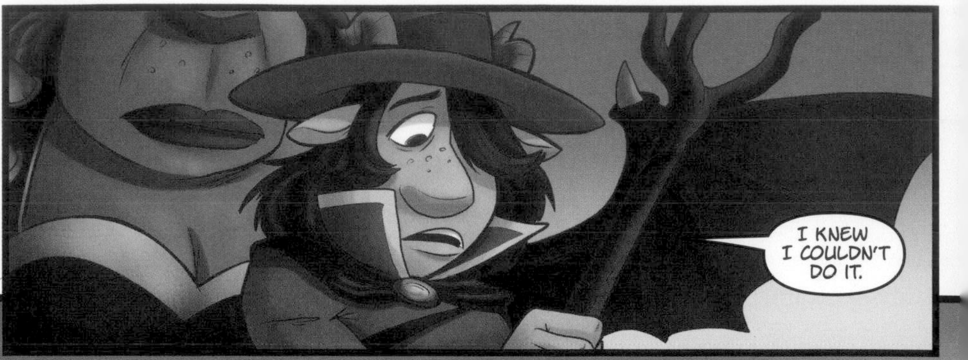
I KNEW I COULDN'T DO IT.

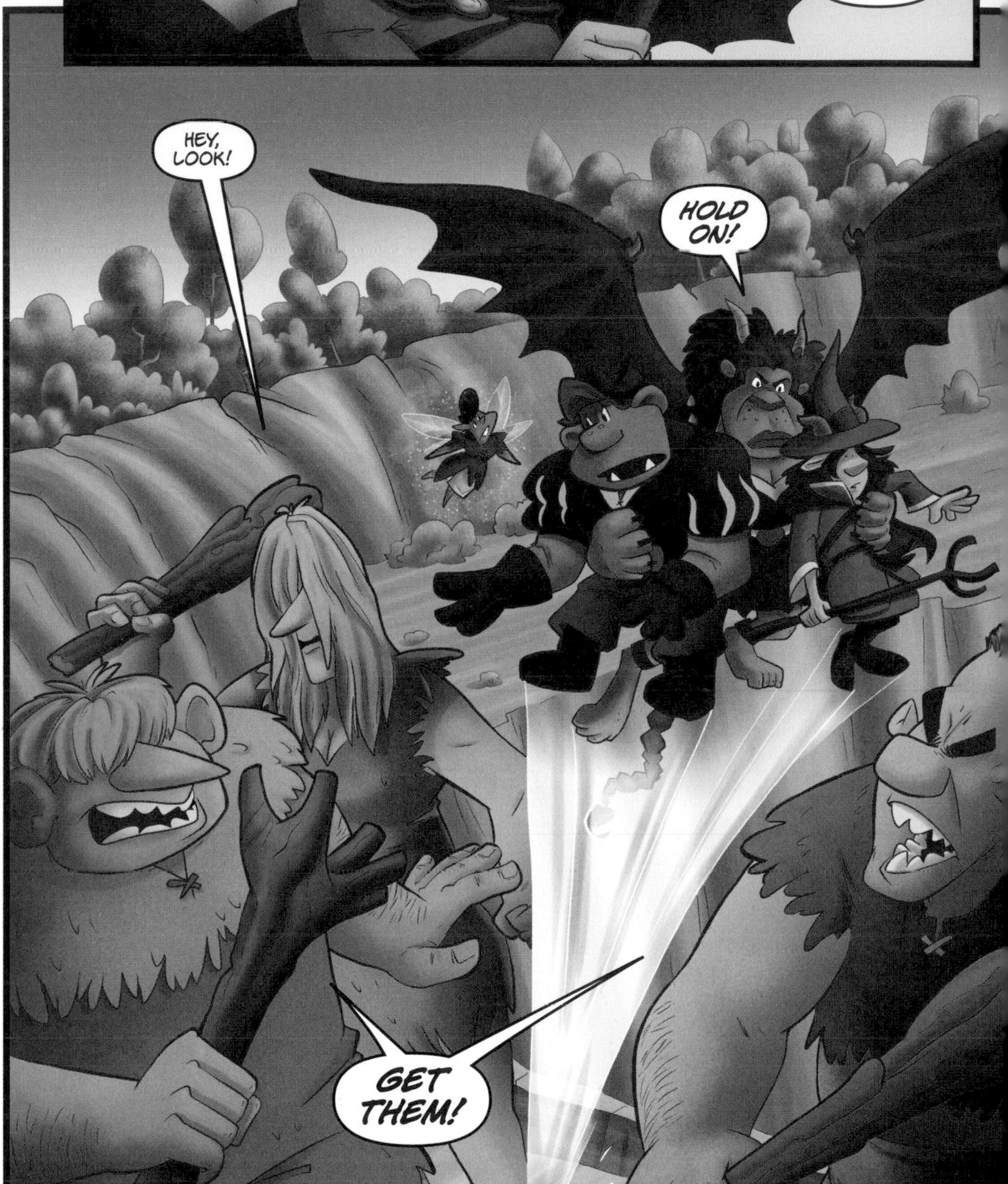
HEY, LOOK!
HOLD ON!
GET THEM!

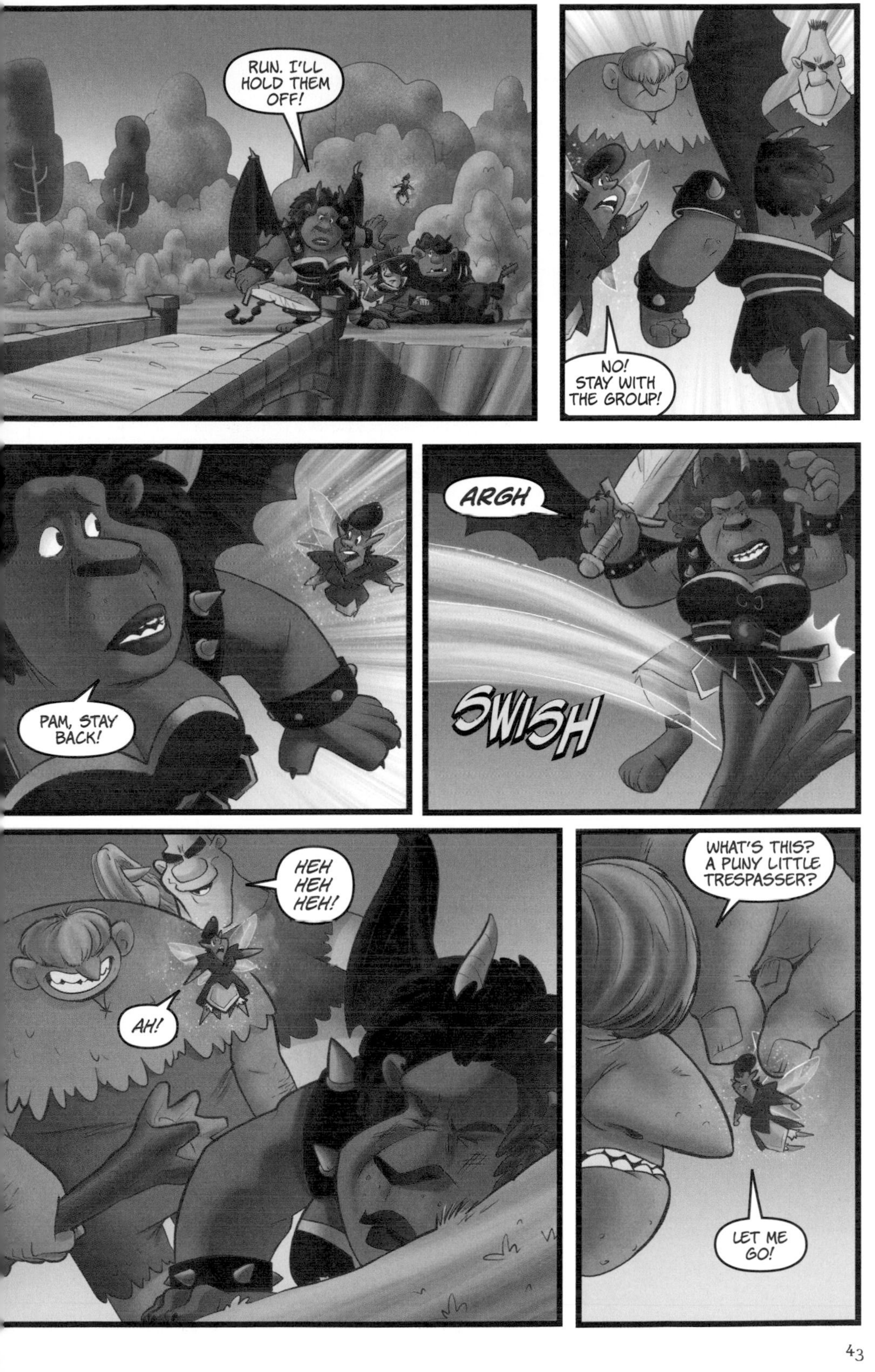

RUN. I'LL HOLD THEM OFF!
NO! STAY WITH THE GROUP!
PAM, STAY BACK!
ARGH
SWISH
HEH HEH HEH!
AH!
WHAT'S THIS? A PUNY LITTLE TRESPASSER?
LET ME GO!

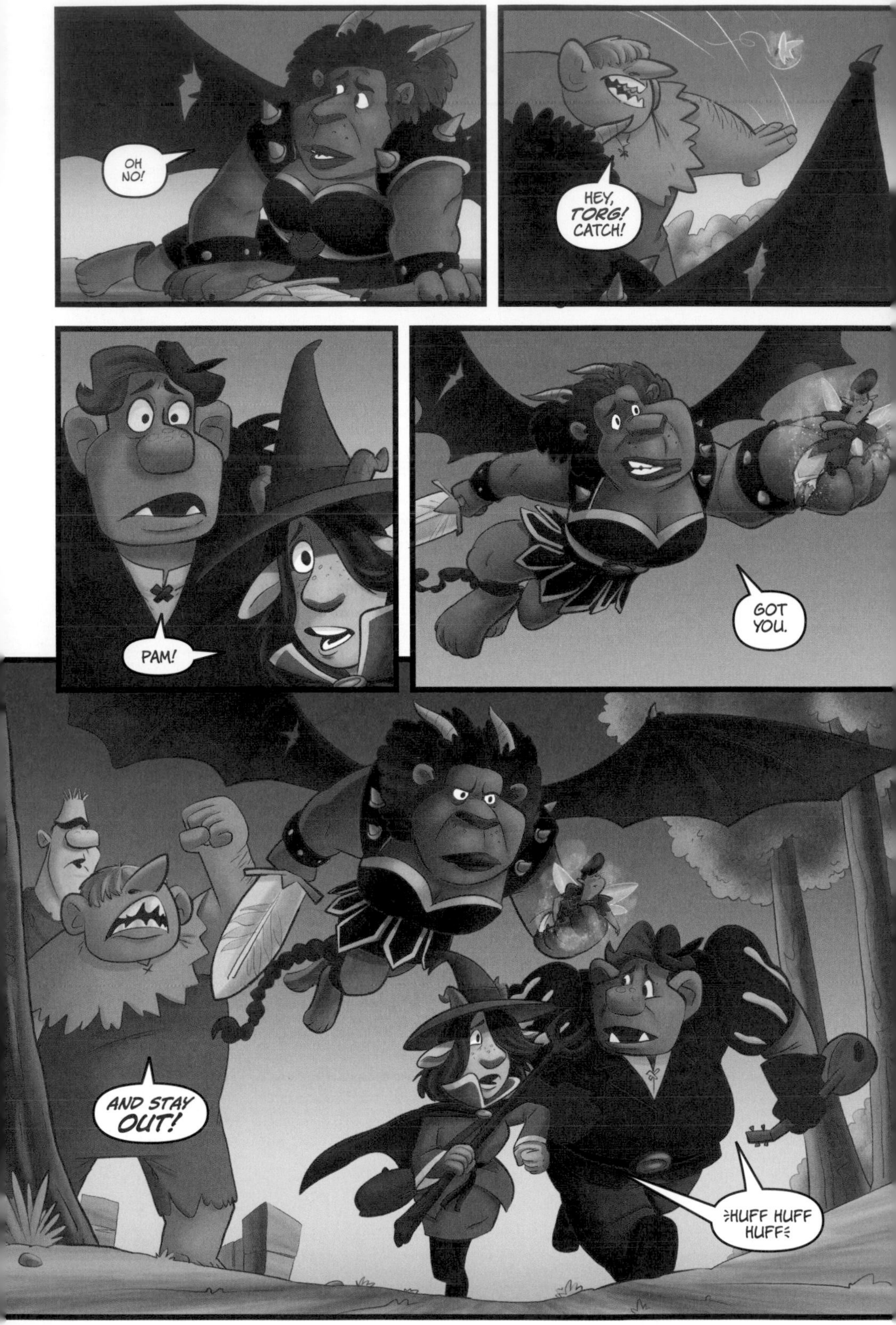
OH NO!
HEY, TORG! CATCH!
PAM!
GOT YOU.
AND STAY OUT!
HUFF HUFF HUFF

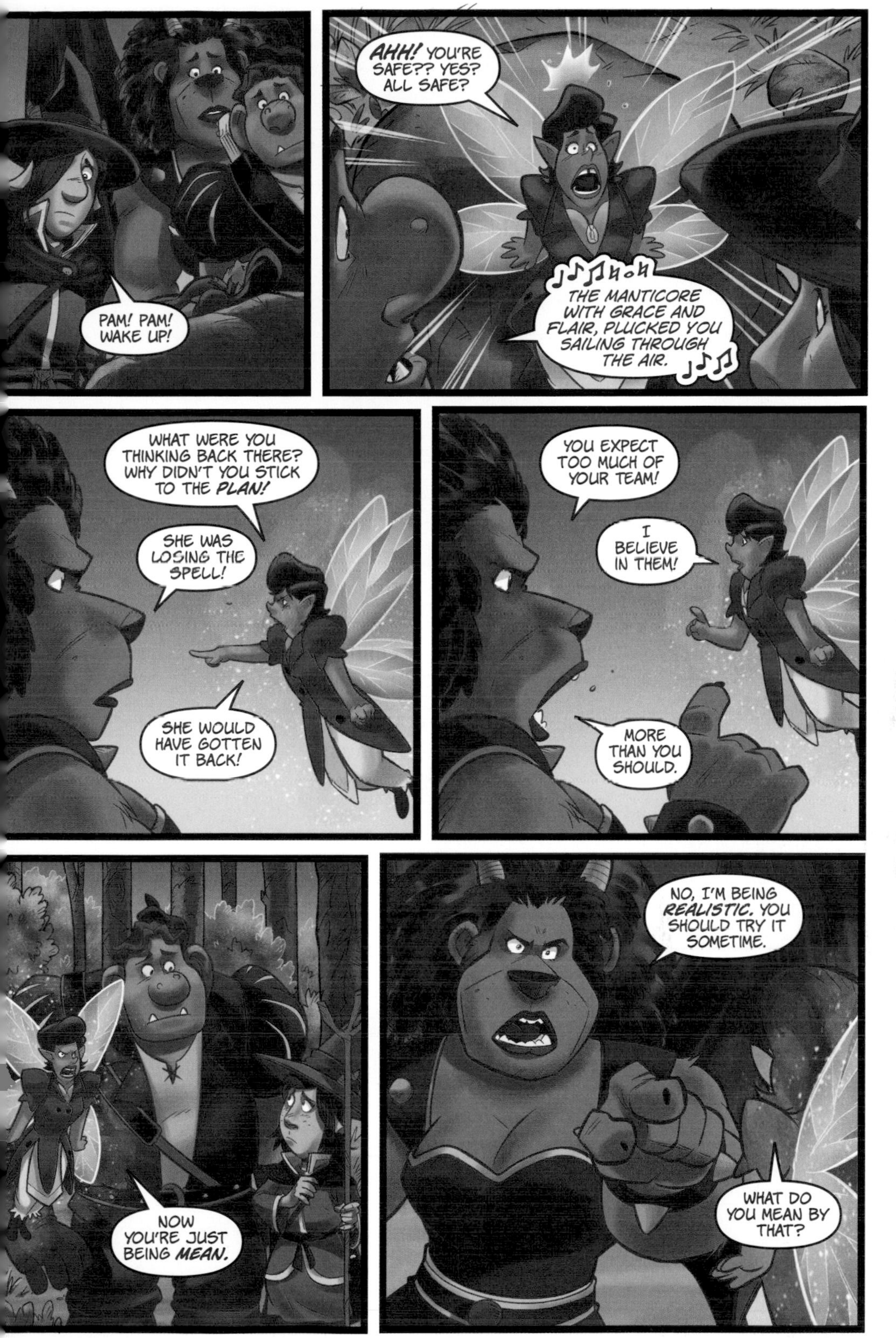
PAM! PAM! WAKE UP!
AHH! YOU'RE SAFE?? YES? ALL SAFE?
THE MANTICORE WITH GRACE AND FLAIR, PLUCKED YOU SAILING THROUGH THE AIR.
WHAT WERE YOU THINKING BACK THERE? WHY DIDN'T YOU STICK TO THE PLAN!
SHE WAS LOSING THE SPELL!
SHE WOULD HAVE GOTTEN IT BACK!
YOU EXPECT TOO MUCH OF YOUR TEAM!
I BELIEVE IN THEM!
MORE THAN YOU SHOULD.
NOW YOU'RE JUST BEING MEAN.
NO, I'M BEING REALISTIC. YOU SHOULD TRY IT SOMETIME.
WHAT DO YOU MEAN BY THAT?

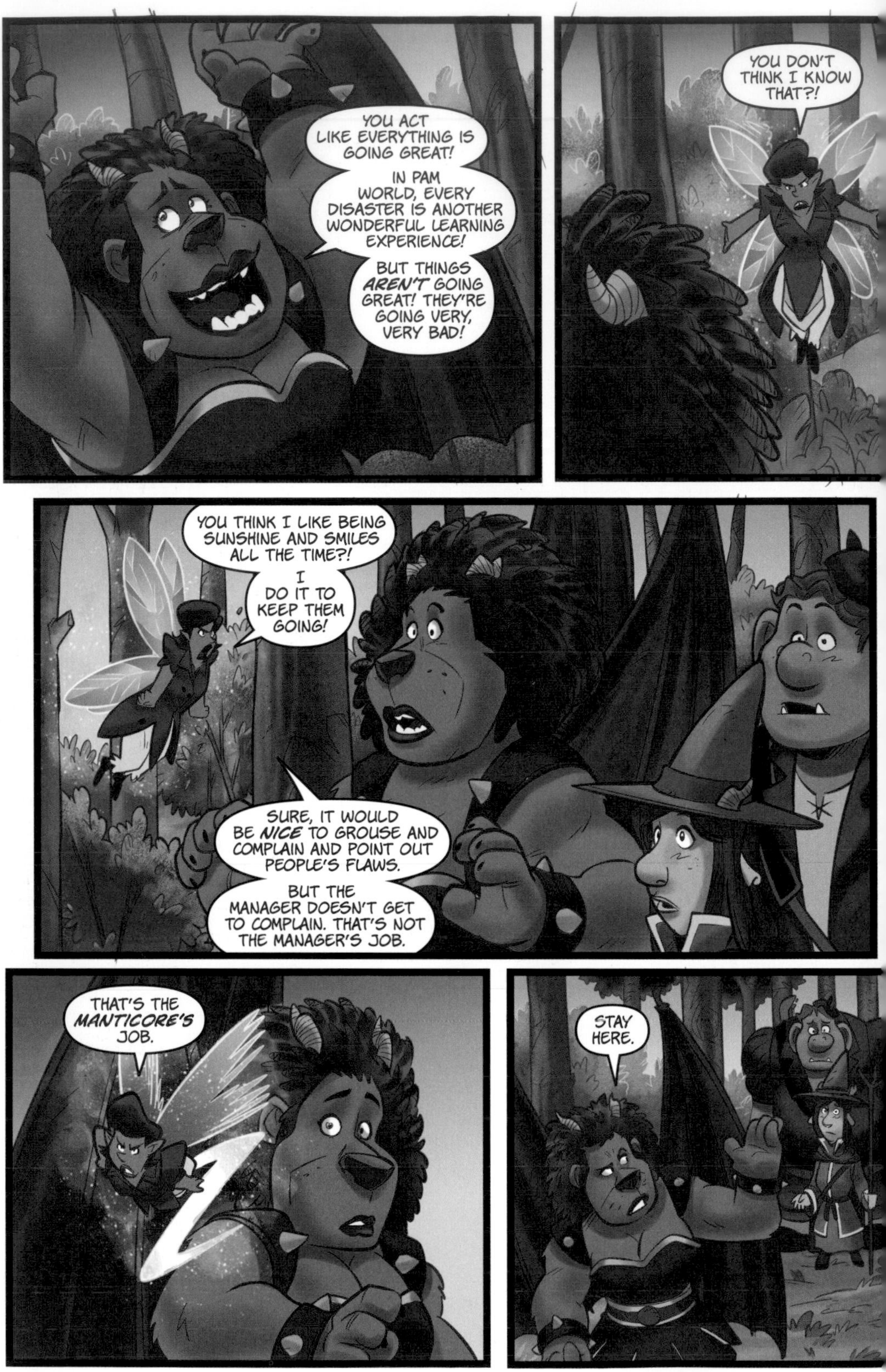
YOU ACT LIKE EVERYTHING IS GOING GREAT!
IN PAM WORLD, EVERY DISASTER IS ANOTHER WONDERFUL LEARNING EXPERIENCE!
BUT THINGS *AREN'T* GOING GREAT! THEY'RE GOING VERY, VERY BAD!
YOU DON'T THINK I KNOW THAT?!
YOU THINK I LIKE BEING SUNSHINE AND SMILES ALL THE TIME?!
I DO IT TO KEEP THEM GOING!
SURE, IT WOULD BE *NICE* TO GROUSE AND COMPLAIN AND POINT OUT PEOPLE'S FLAWS.
BUT THE MANAGER DOESN'T GET TO COMPLAIN. THAT'S NOT THE MANAGER'S JOB.
THAT'S THE *MANTICORE'S* JOB.
STAY HERE.

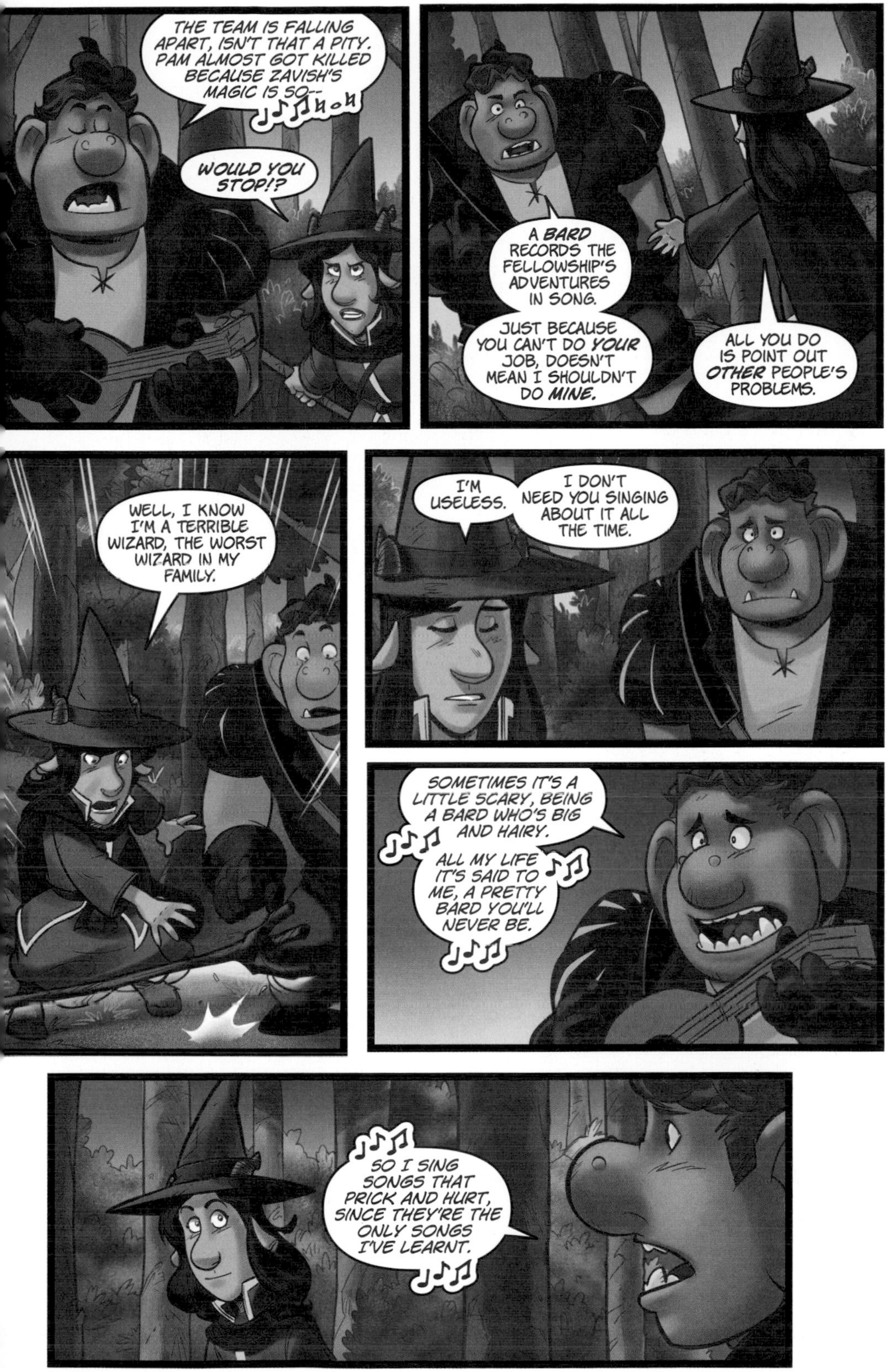
THE TEAM IS FALLING APART, ISN'T THAT A PITY. PAM ALMOST GOT KILLED BECAUSE ZAVISH'S MAGIC IS SO--
WOULD YOU STOP!?
A BARD RECORDS THE FELLOWSHIP'S ADVENTURES IN SONG.
JUST BECAUSE YOU CAN'T DO YOUR JOB, DOESN'T MEAN I SHOULDN'T DO MINE.
ALL YOU DO IS POINT OUT OTHER PEOPLE'S PROBLEMS.
WELL, I KNOW I'M A TERRIBLE WIZARD, THE WORST WIZARD IN MY FAMILY.
I'M USELESS.
I DON'T NEED YOU SINGING ABOUT IT ALL THE TIME.
SOMETIMES IT'S A LITTLE SCARY, BEING A BARD WHO'S BIG AND HAIRY.
ALL MY LIFE IT'S SAID TO ME, A PRETTY BARD YOU'LL NEVER BE.
SO I SING SONGS THAT PRICK AND HURT, SINCE THEY'RE THE ONLY SONGS I'VE LEARNT.

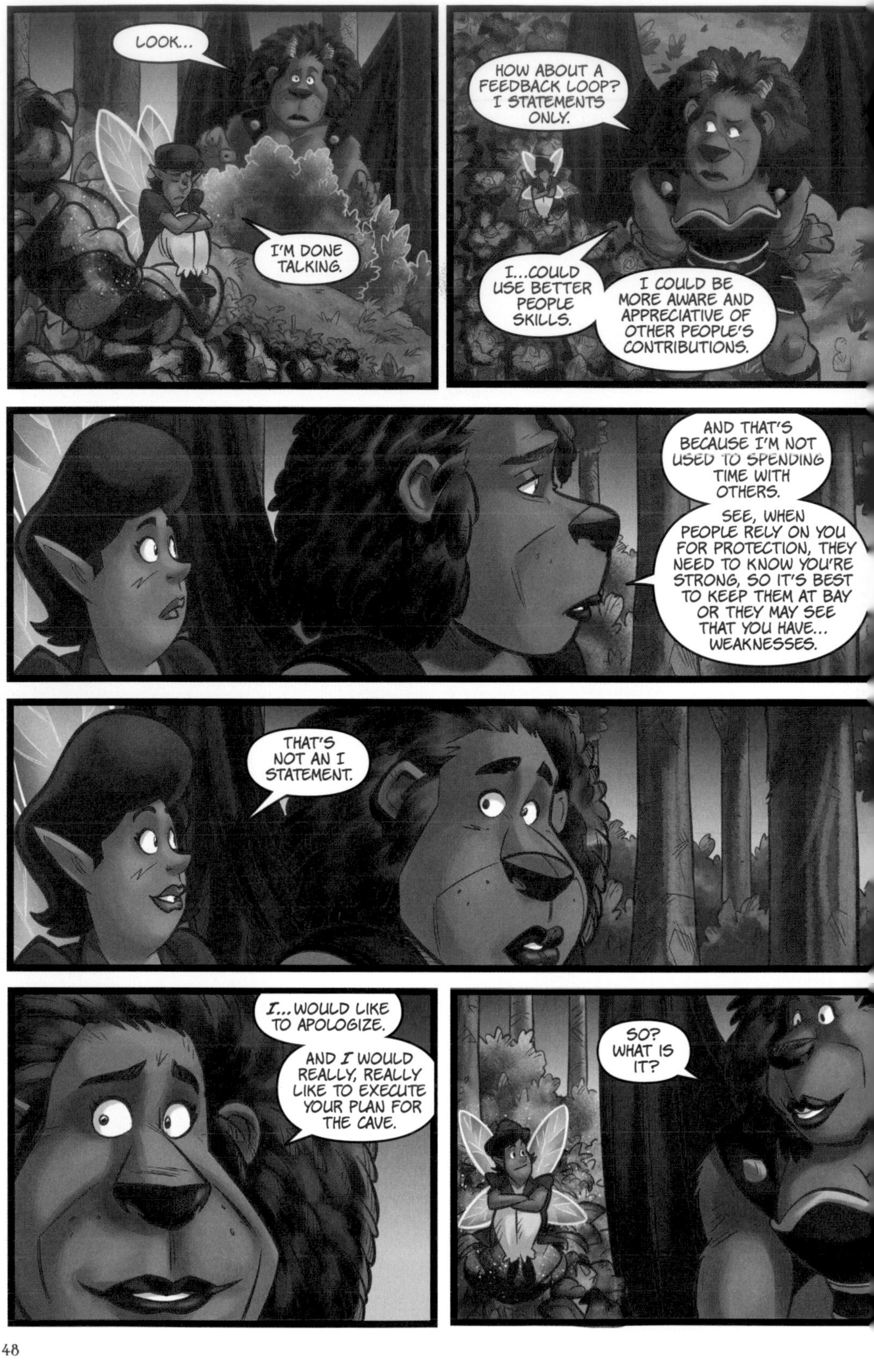
LOOK...
I'M DONE TALKING.
HOW ABOUT A FEEDBACK LOOP? I STATEMENTS ONLY.
I...COULD USE BETTER PEOPLE SKILLS.
I COULD BE MORE AWARE AND APPRECIATIVE OF OTHER PEOPLE'S CONTRIBUTIONS.
AND THAT'S BECAUSE I'M NOT USED TO SPENDING TIME WITH OTHERS.
SEE, WHEN PEOPLE RELY ON YOU FOR PROTECTION, THEY NEED TO KNOW YOU'RE STRONG, SO IT'S BEST TO KEEP THEM AT BAY OR THEY MAY SEE THAT YOU HAVE... WEAKNESSES.
THAT'S NOT AN I STATEMENT.
I...WOULD LIKE TO APOLOGIZE.
AND I WOULD REALLY, REALLY LIKE TO EXECUTE YOUR PLAN FOR THE CAVE.
SO? WHAT IS IT?

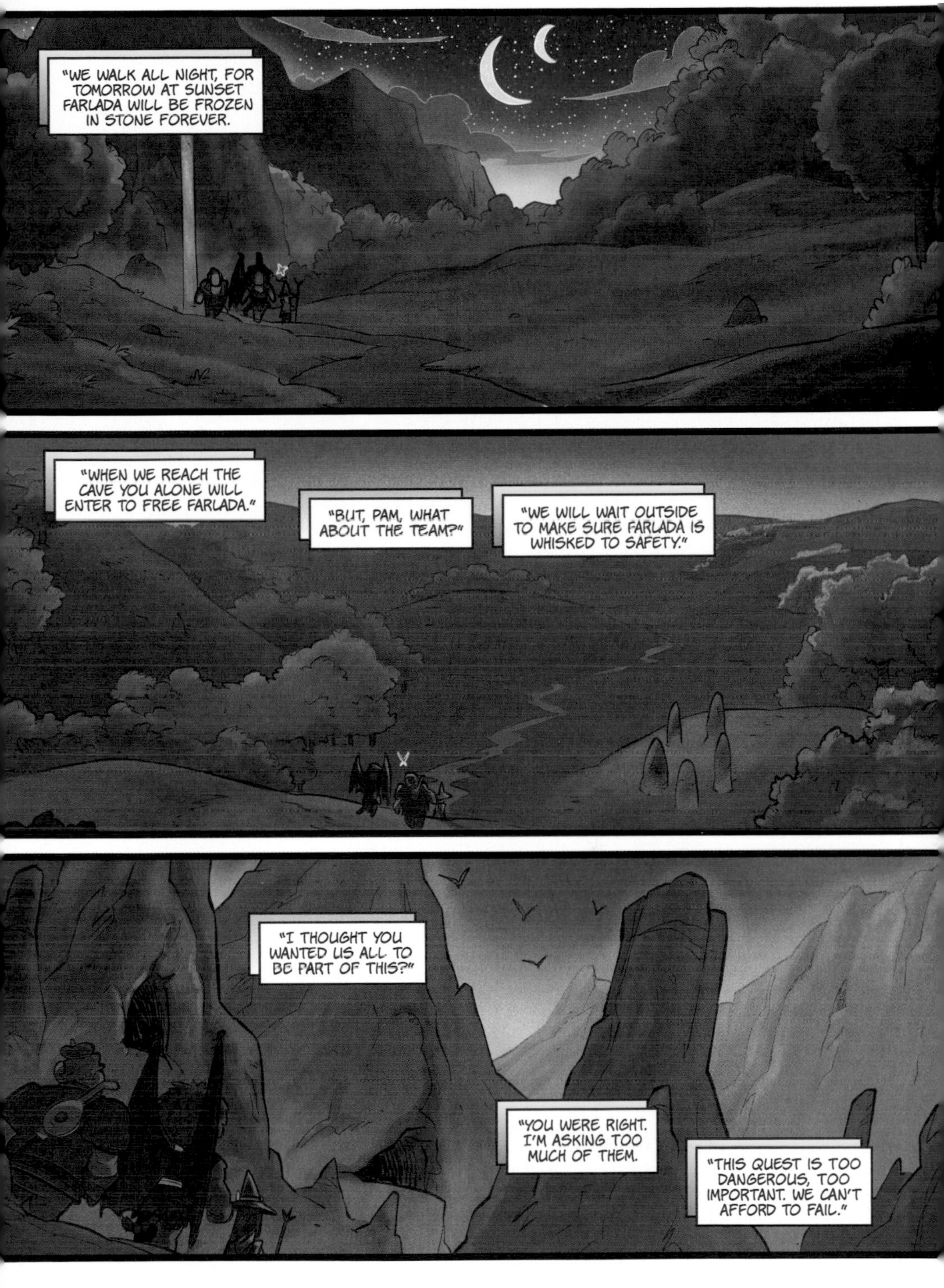
"WE WALK ALL NIGHT, FOR TOMORROW AT SUNSET FARLADA WILL BE FROZEN IN STONE FOREVER.
"WHEN WE REACH THE CAVE YOU ALONE WILL ENTER TO FREE FARLADA."
"BUT, PAM, WHAT ABOUT THE TEAM?"
"WE WILL WAIT OUTSIDE TO MAKE SURE FARLADA IS WHISKED TO SAFETY."
"I THOUGHT YOU WANTED US ALL TO BE PART OF THIS?"
"YOU WERE RIGHT. I'M ASKING TOO MUCH OF THEM.
"THIS QUEST IS TOO DANGEROUS, TOO IMPORTANT. WE CAN'T AFFORD TO FAIL."

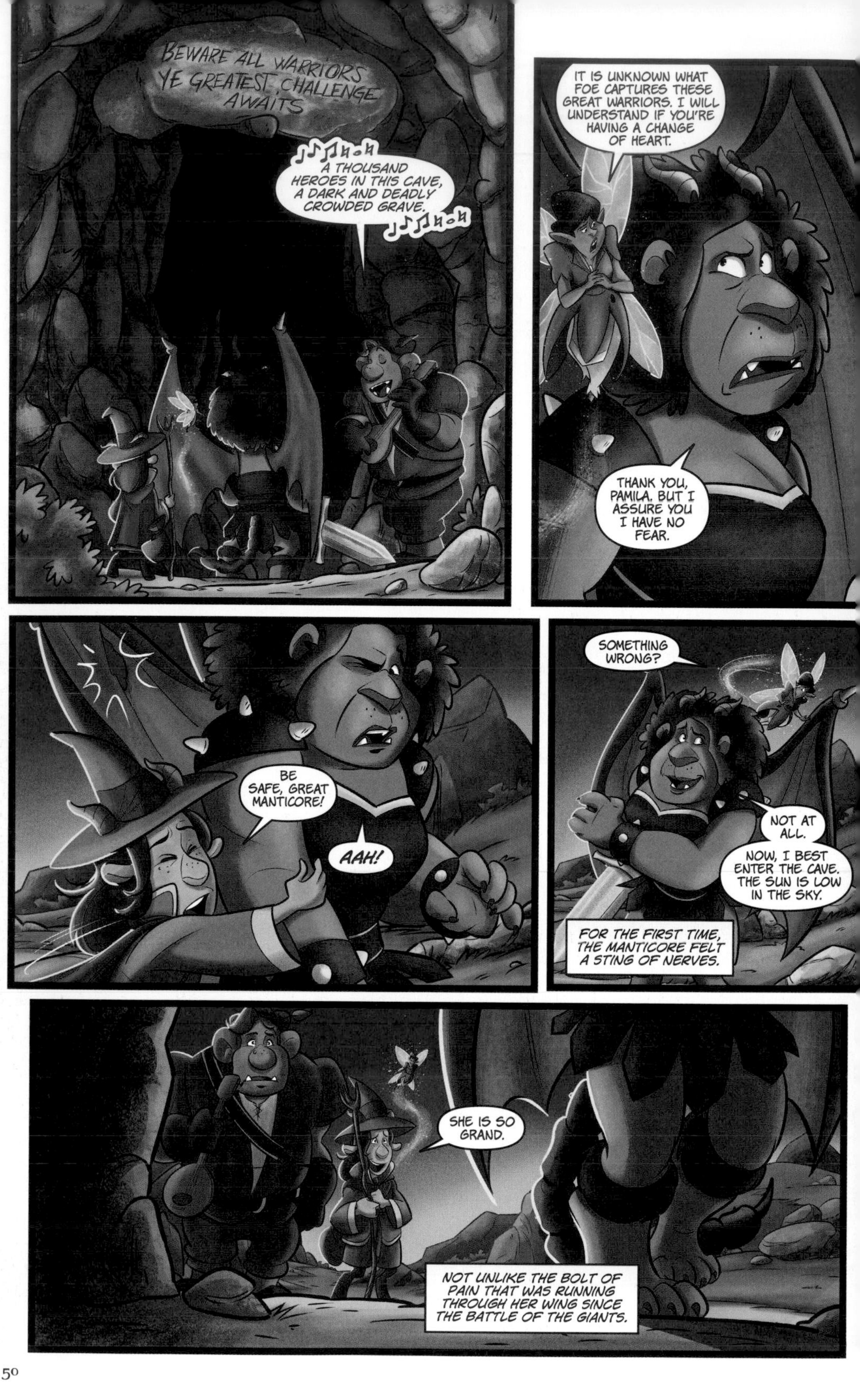
BEWARE ALL WARRIORS YE GREATEST CHALLENGE AWAITS
A THOUSAND HEROES IN THIS CAVE, A DARK AND DEADLY CROWDED GRAVE.
IT IS UNKNOWN WHAT FOE CAPTURES THESE GREAT WARRIORS. I WILL UNDERSTAND IF YOU'RE HAVING A CHANGE OF HEART.
THANK YOU, PAMILA, BUT I ASSURE YOU I HAVE NO FEAR.
BE SAFE, GREAT MANTICORE!
AAH!
SOMETHING WRONG?
NOT AT ALL.
NOW, I BEST ENTER THE CAVE. THE SUN IS LOW IN THE SKY.
FOR THE FIRST TIME, THE MANTICORE FELT A STING OF NERVES.
SHE IS SO GRAND.
NOT UNLIKE THE BOLT OF PAIN THAT WAS RUNNING THROUGH HER WING SINCE THE BATTLE OF THE GIANTS.

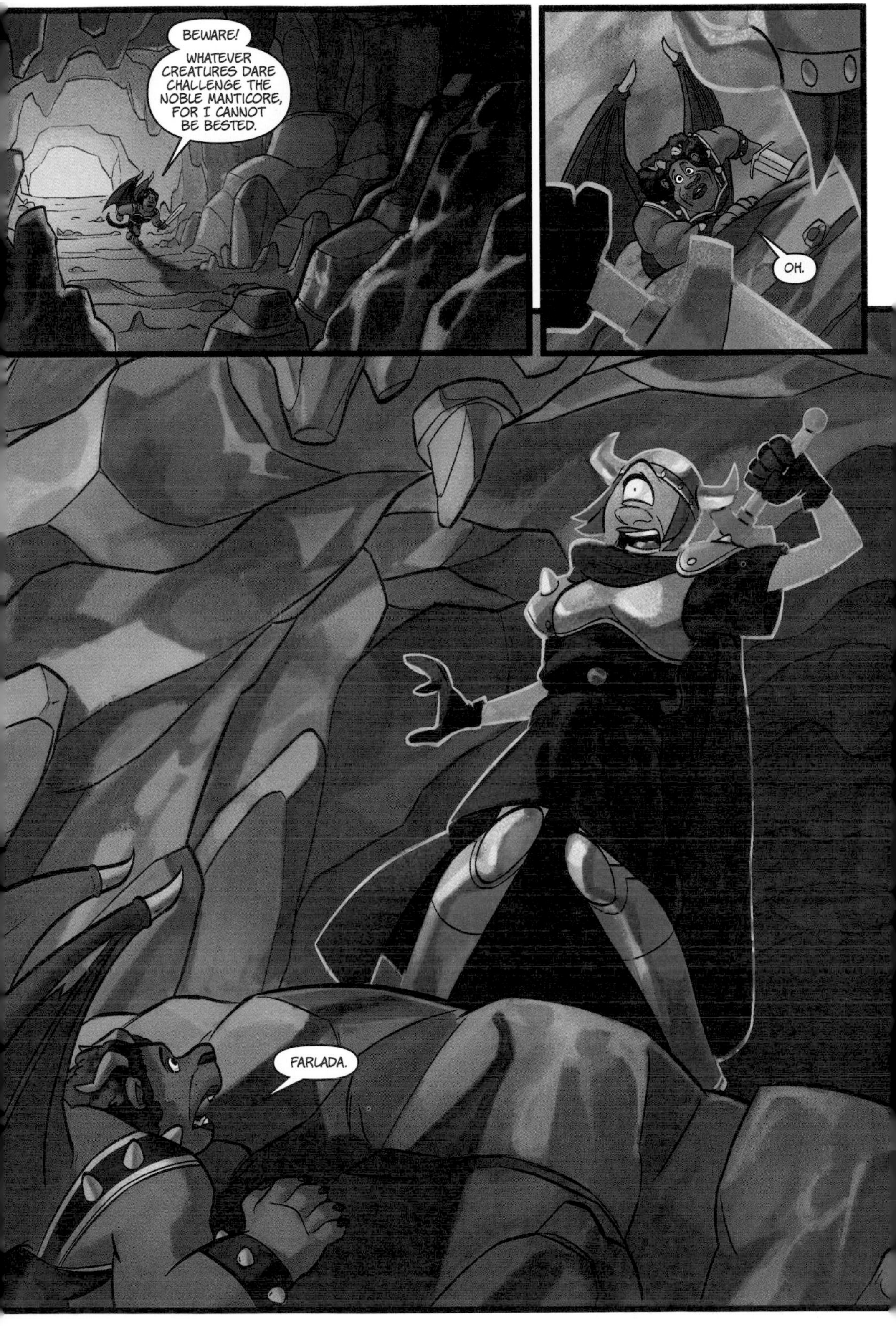
BEWARE!
WHATEVER CREATURES DARE CHALLENGE THE NOBLE MANTICORE, FOR I CANNOT BE BESTED.
OH.
FARLADA.

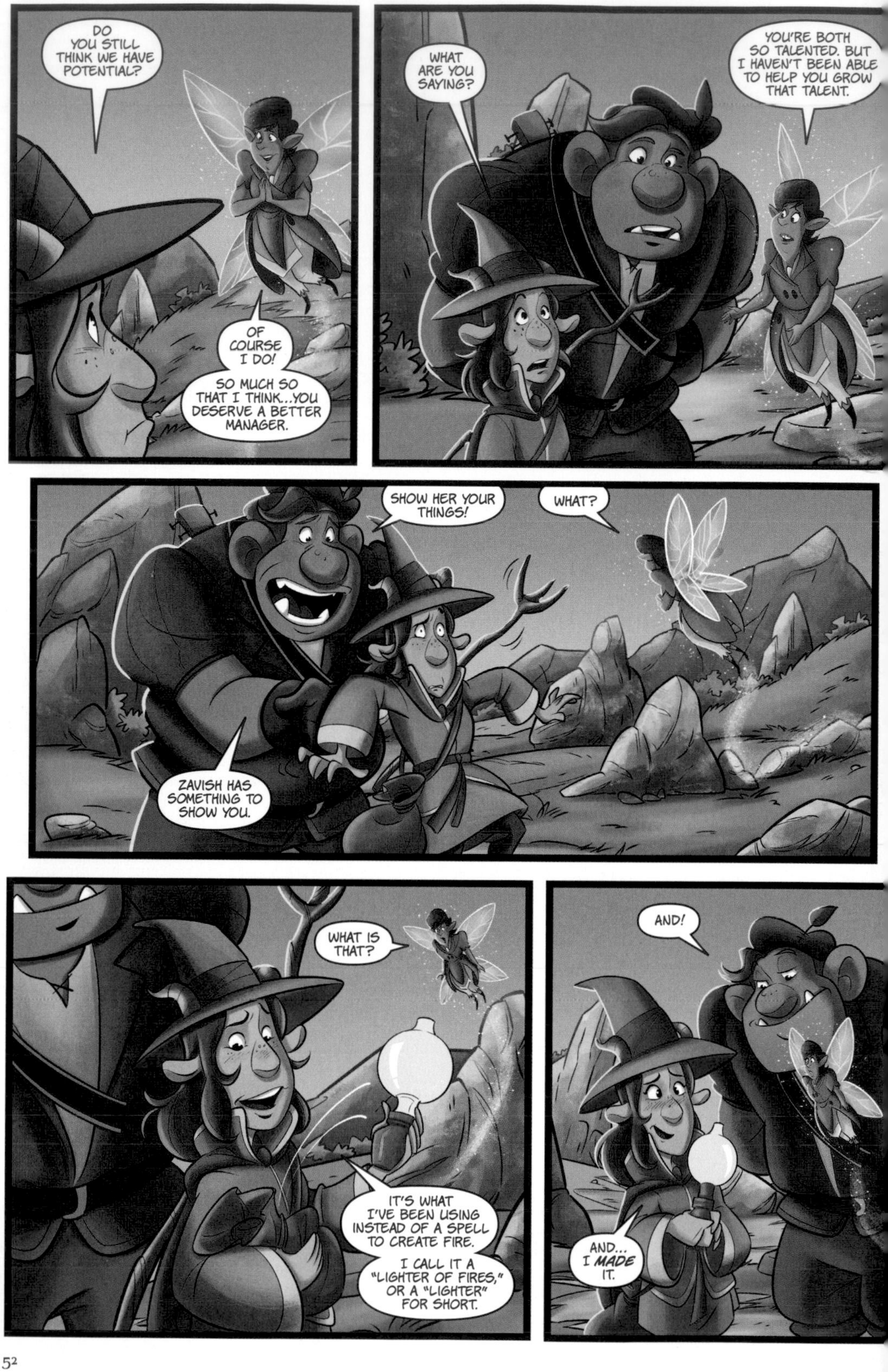
DO YOU STILL THINK WE HAVE POTENTIAL?
OF COURSE I DO!
SO MUCH SO THAT I THINK...YOU DESERVE A BETTER MANAGER.
WHAT ARE YOU SAYING?
YOU'RE BOTH SO TALENTED. BUT I HAVEN'T BEEN ABLE TO HELP YOU GROW THAT TALENT.
SHOW HER YOUR THINGS!
WHAT?
ZAVISH HAS SOMETHING TO SHOW YOU.
WHAT IS THAT?
IT'S WHAT I'VE BEEN USING INSTEAD OF A SPELL TO CREATE FIRE.
I CALL IT A "LIGHTER OF FIRES," OR A "LIGHTER" FOR SHORT.
AND!
AND... I *MADE* IT.

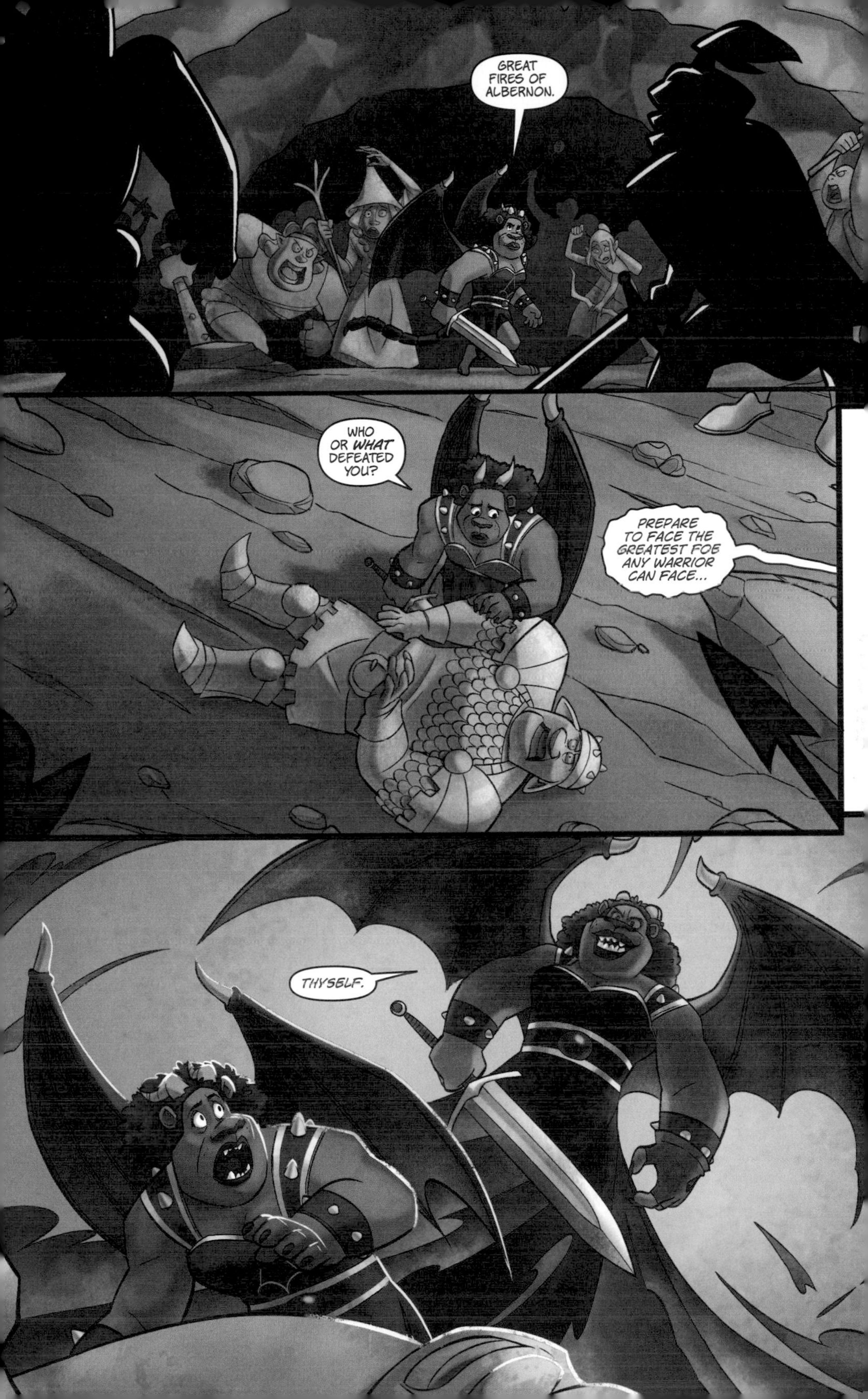
GREAT FIRES OF ALBERNON.
WHO OR *WHAT* DEFEATED YOU?
PREPARE TO FACE THE GREATEST FOE ANY WARRIOR CAN FACE...
THYSELF.

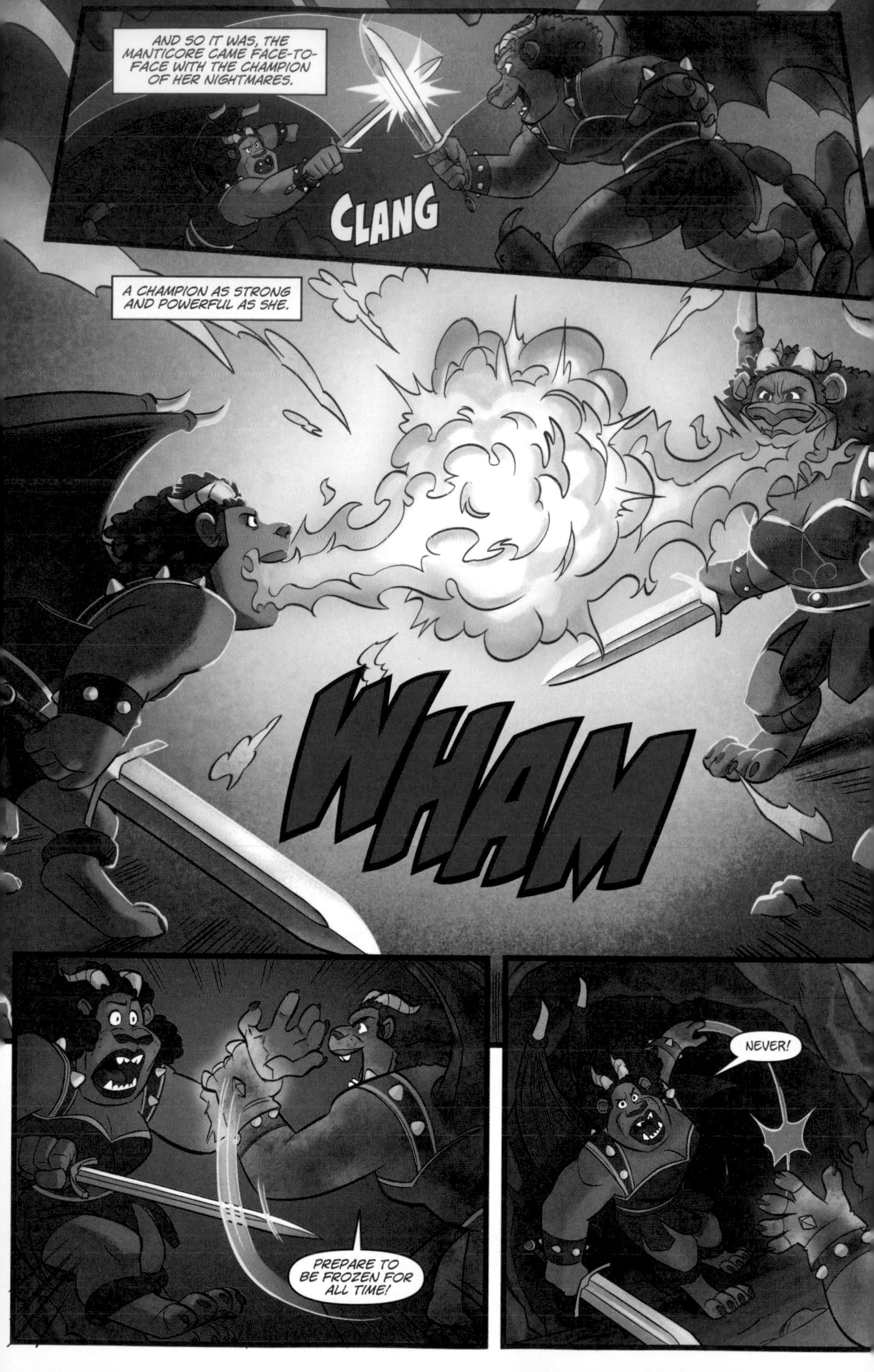
AND SO IT WAS, THE MANTICORE CAME FACE-TO-FACE WITH THE CHAMPION OF HER NIGHTMARES.
CLANG
A CHAMPION AS STRONG AND POWERFUL AS SHE.
WHAM
PREPARE TO BE FROZEN FOR ALL TIME!
NEVER!

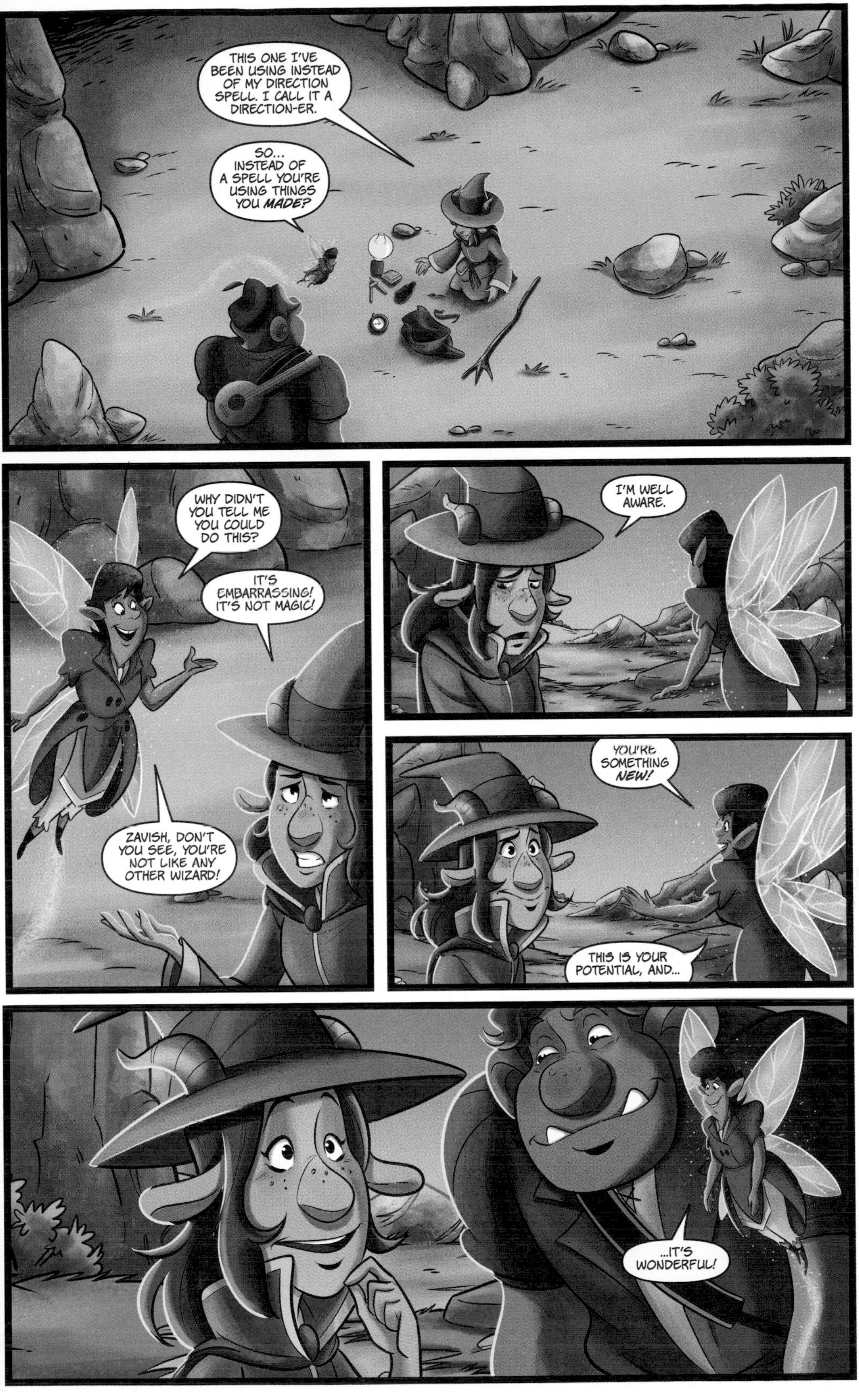

THIS ONE I'VE BEEN USING INSTEAD OF MY DIRECTION SPELL. I CALL IT A DIRECTION-ER.
SO... INSTEAD OF A SPELL YOU'RE USING THINGS YOU *MADE?*
WHY DIDN'T YOU TELL ME YOU COULD DO THIS?
IT'S EMBARRASSING! IT'S NOT MAGIC!
ZAVISH, DON'T YOU SEE, YOU'RE NOT LIKE ANY OTHER WIZARD!
I'M WELL AWARE.
YOU'RE SOMETHING *NEW!*
THIS IS YOUR POTENTIAL, AND...
...IT'S WONDERFUL!

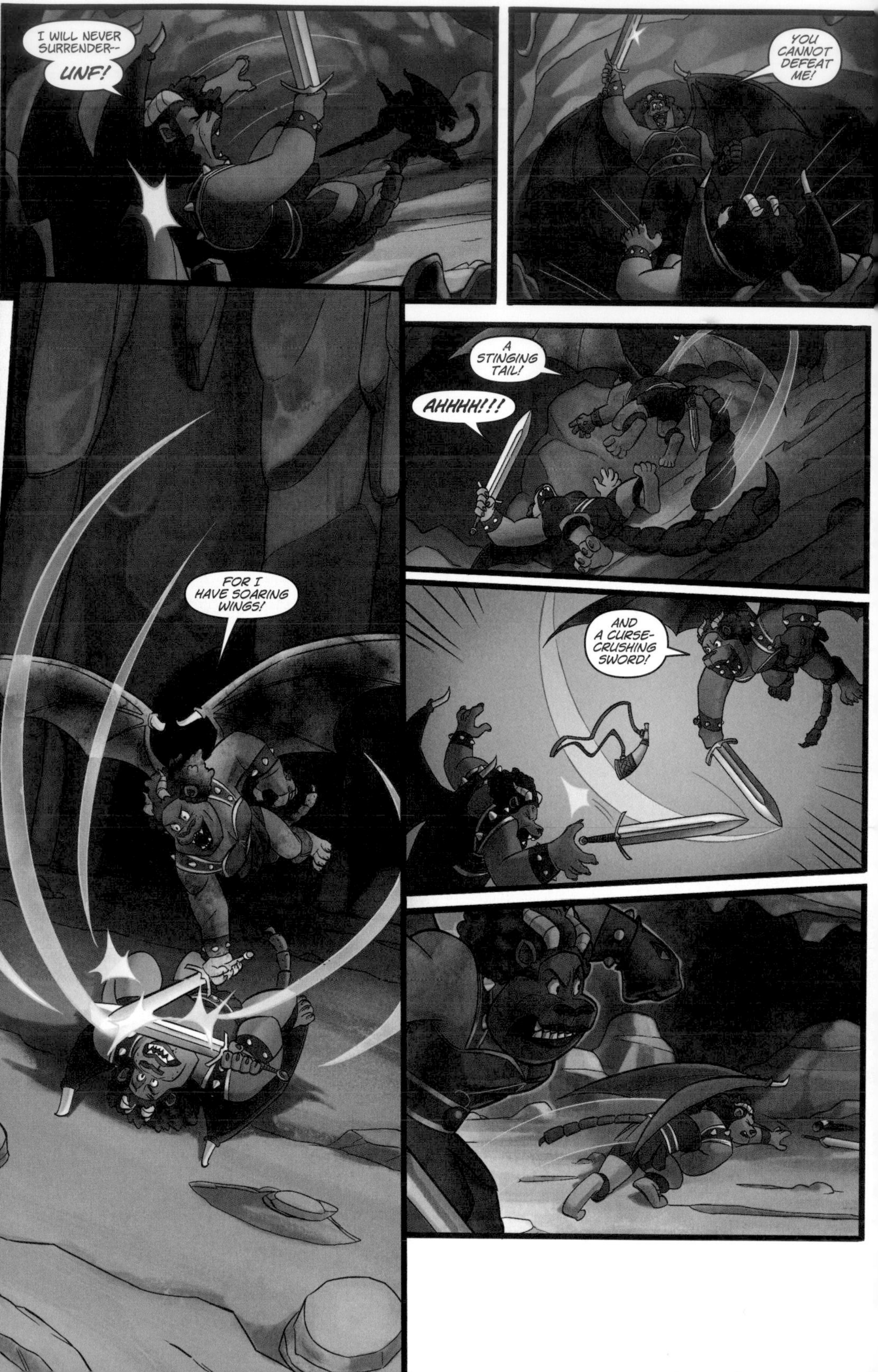
I WILL NEVER SURRENDER--
UNF!
YOU CANNOT DEFEAT ME!
FOR I HAVE SOARING WINGS!
A STINGING TAIL!
AHHHH!!!
AND A CURSE-CRUSHING SWORD!

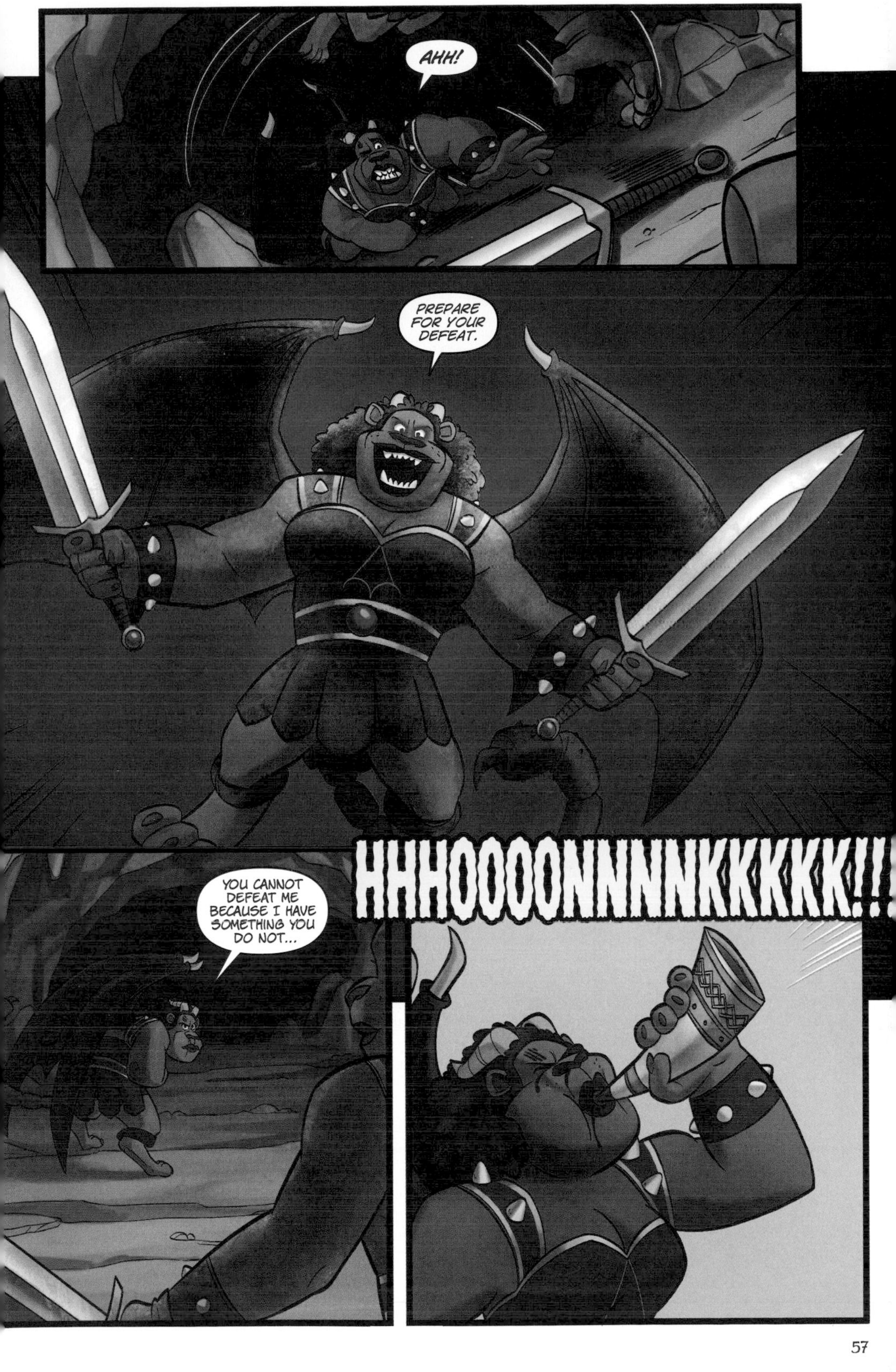
AHH!
PREPARE FOR YOUR DEFEAT.
YOU CANNOT DEFEAT ME BECAUSE I HAVE SOMETHING YOU DO NOT...
HHHOOOONNNNKKKKK!!

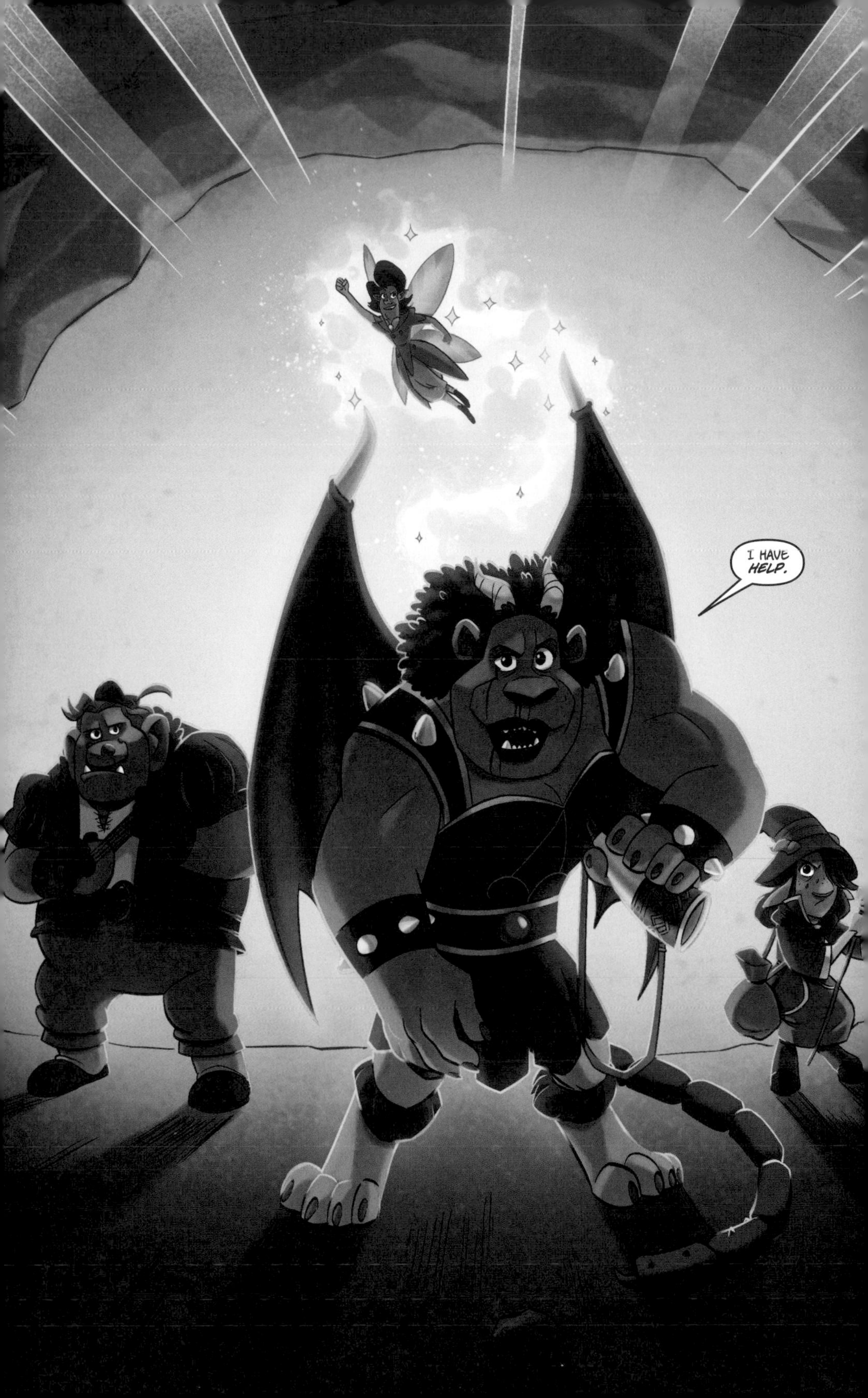
I HAVE HELP.

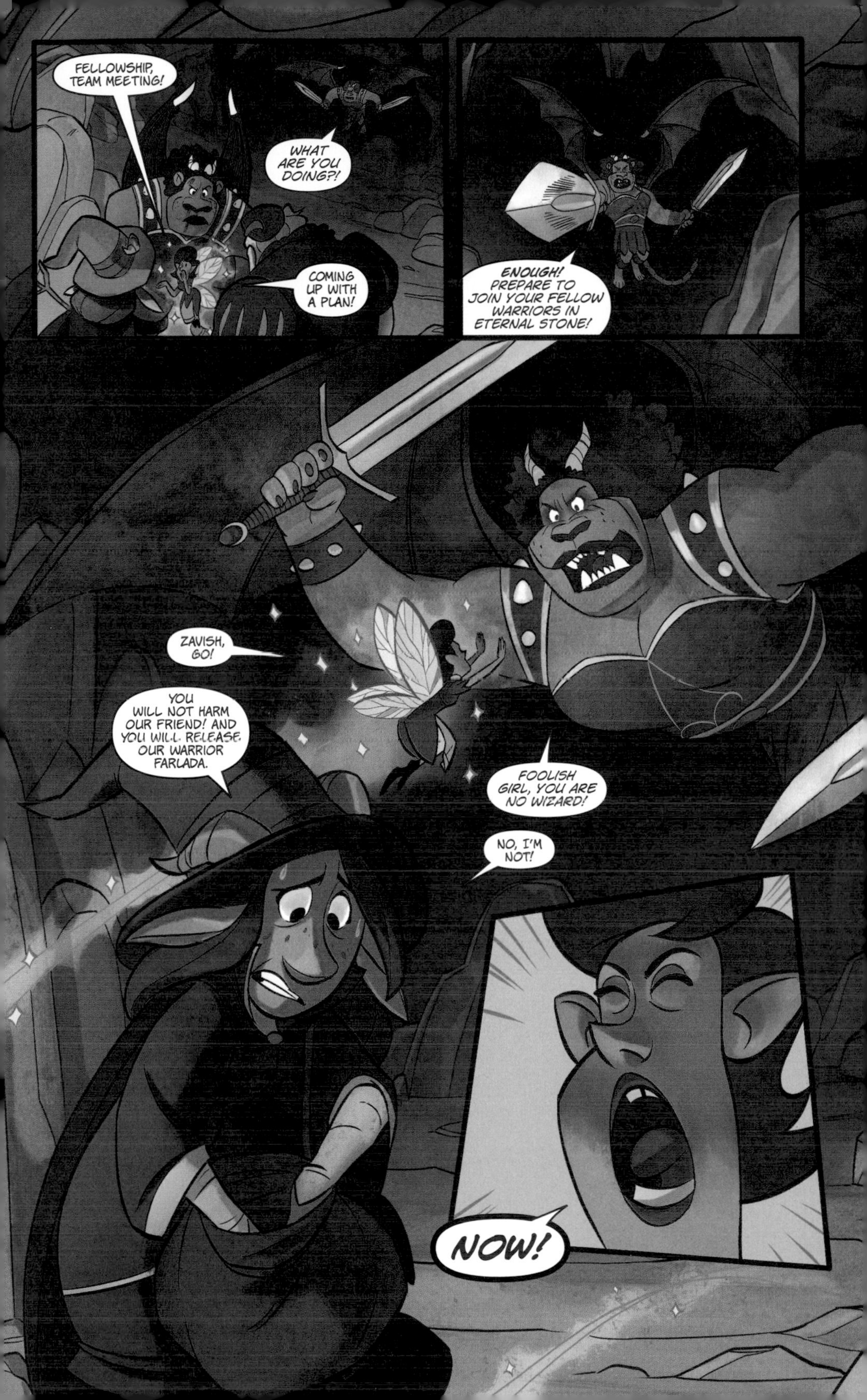
FELLOWSHIP, TEAM MEETING!
WHAT ARE YOU DOING?!
COMING UP WITH A PLAN!
ENOUGH! PREPARE TO JOIN YOUR FELLOW WARRIORS IN ETERNAL STONE!
ZAVISH, GO!
YOU WILL NOT HARM OUR FRIEND! AND YOU WILL RELEASE OUR WARRIOR FARLADA.
FOOLISH GIRL, YOU ARE NO WIZARD!
NO, I'M NOT!
NOW!

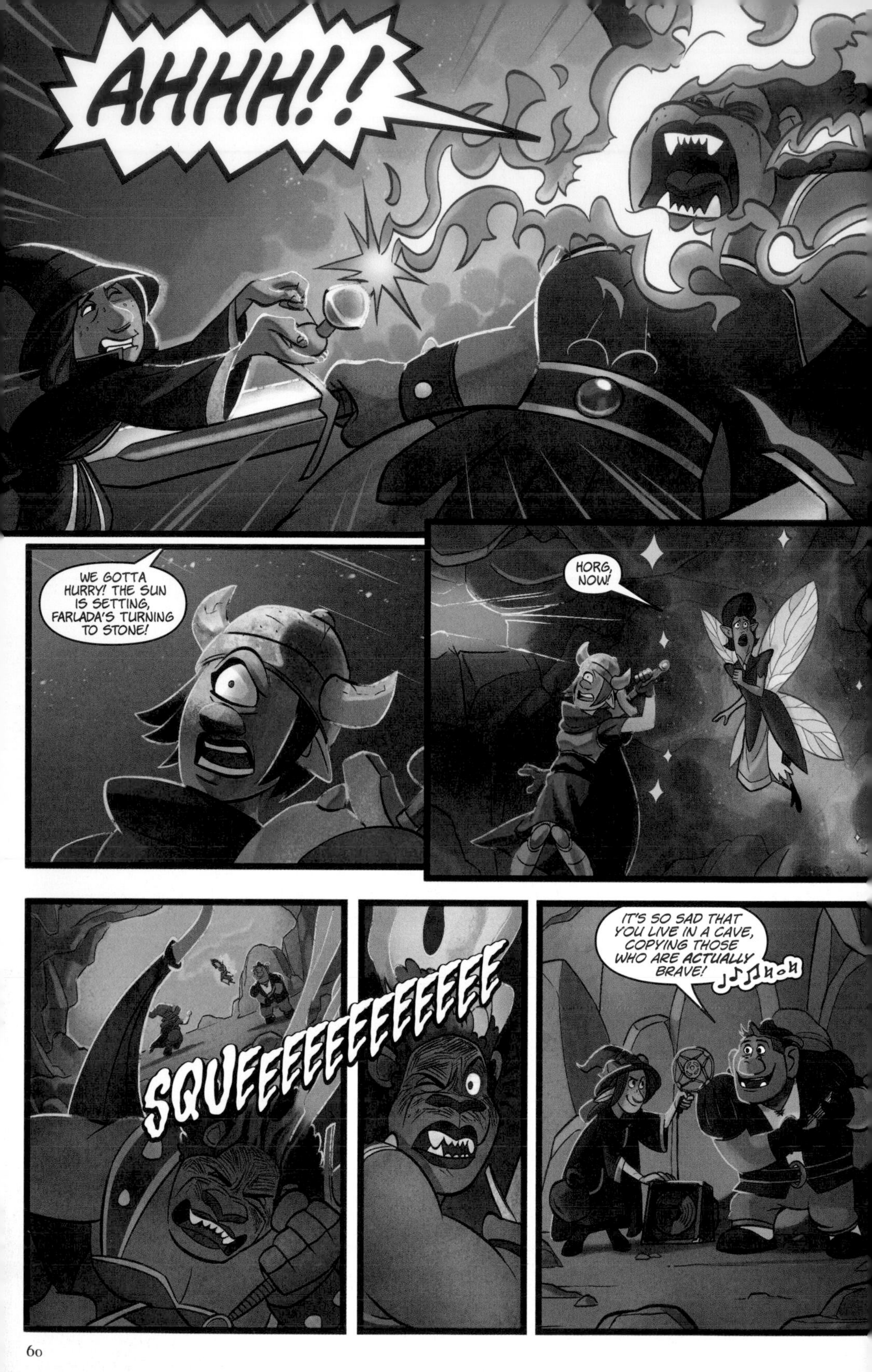
AHHH!!
WE GOTTA HURRY! THE SUN IS SETTING, FARLADA'S TURNING TO STONE!
HORG, NOW!
SQUEEEEEEEEEEEEEE
IT'S SO SAD THAT YOU LIVE IN A CAVE, COPYING THOSE WHO ARE ACTUALLY BRAVE!

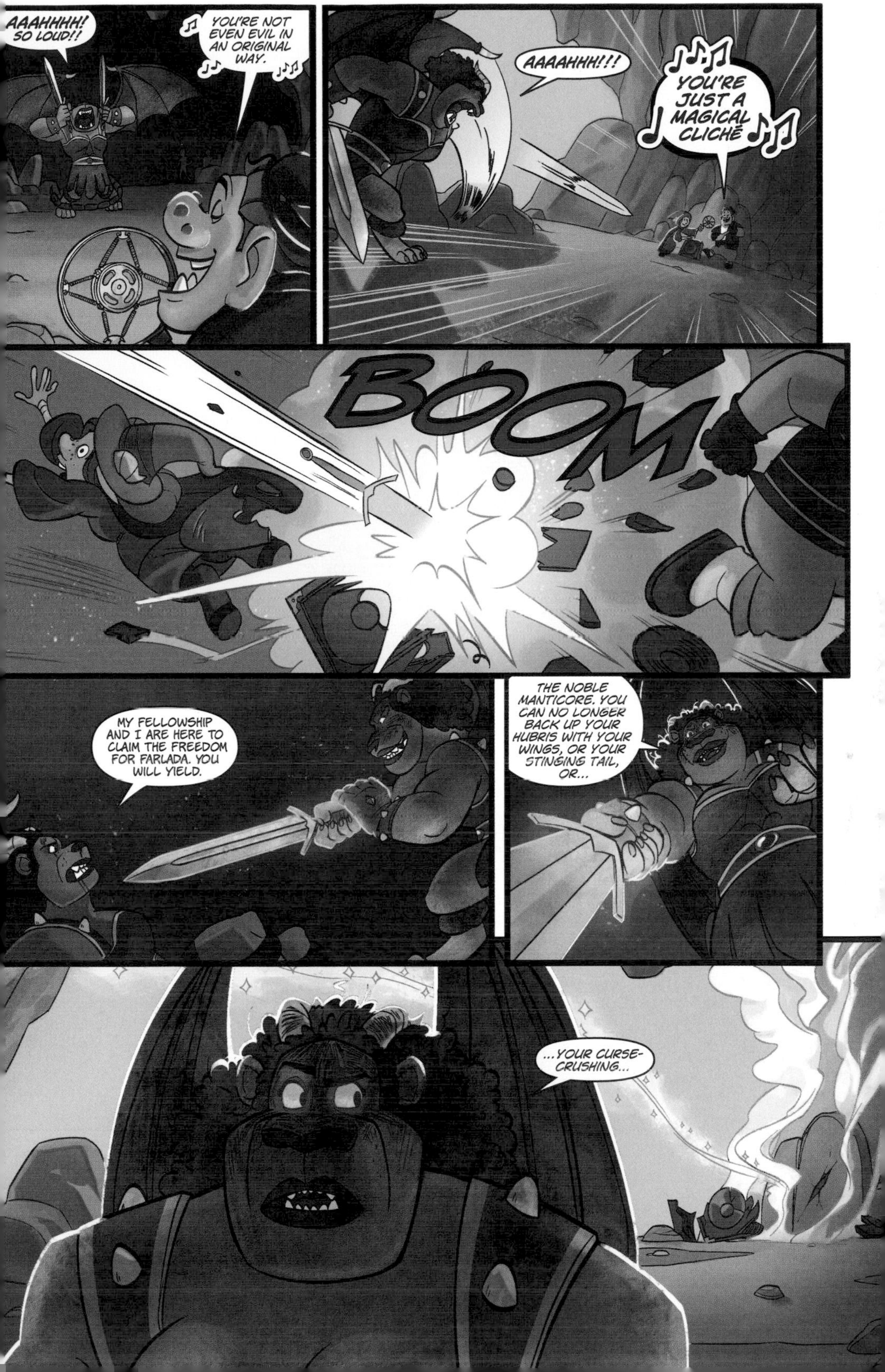
AAAHHHH! SO LOUD!!
YOU'RE NOT EVEN EVIL IN AN ORIGINAL WAY.
AAAAHHH!!!
YOU'RE JUST A MAGICAL CLICHÉ
BOOM
MY FELLOWSHIP AND I ARE HERE TO CLAIM THE FREEDOM FOR FARLADA. YOU WILL YIELD.
THE NOBLE MANTICORE. YOU CAN NO LONGER BACK UP YOUR HUBRIS WITH YOUR WINGS, OR YOUR STINGING TAIL, OR...
...YOUR CURSE-CRUSHING...

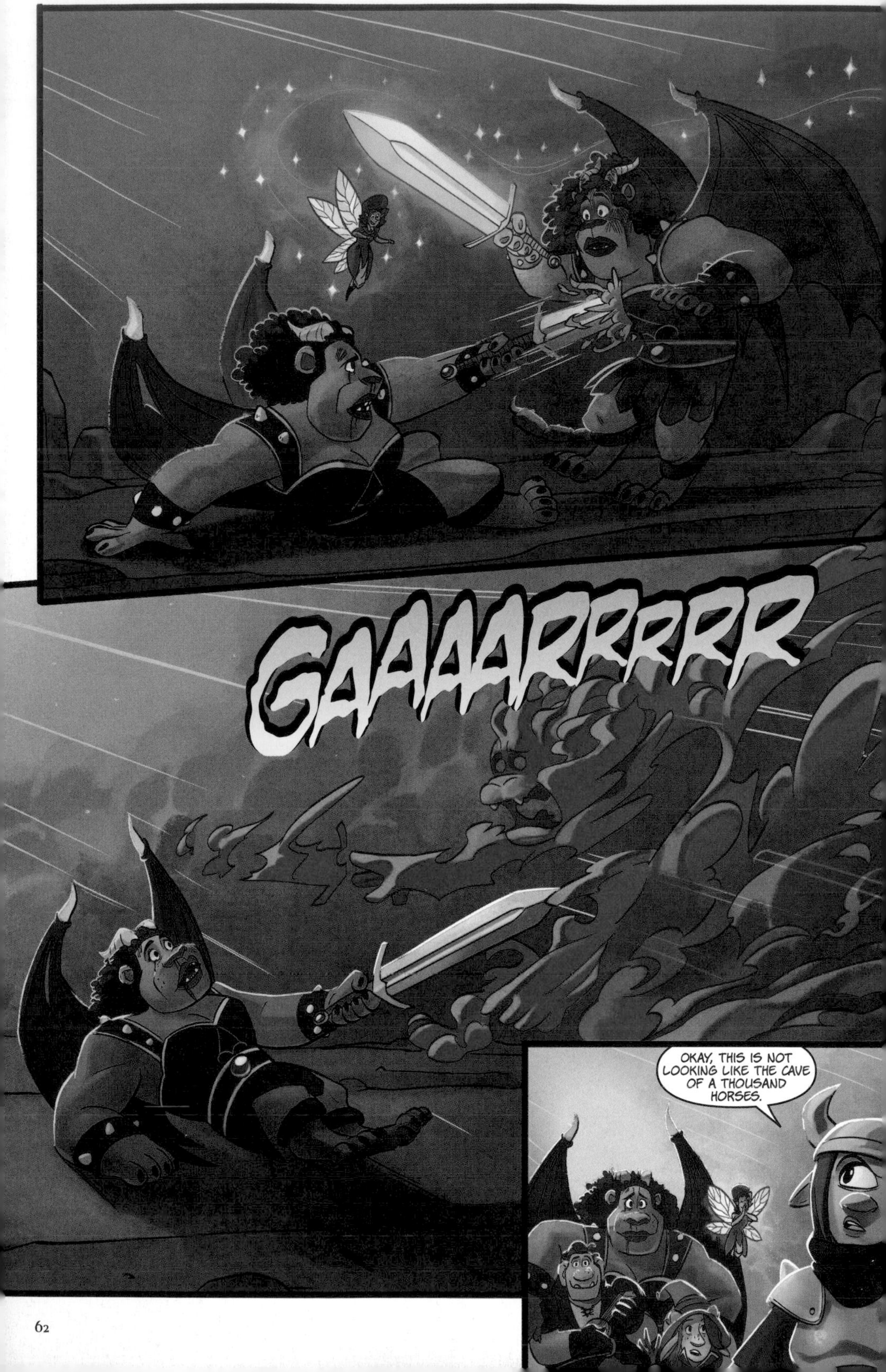
GAAAARRRRR
OKAY, THIS IS NOT LOOKING LIKE THE CAVE OF A THOUSAND HORSES.

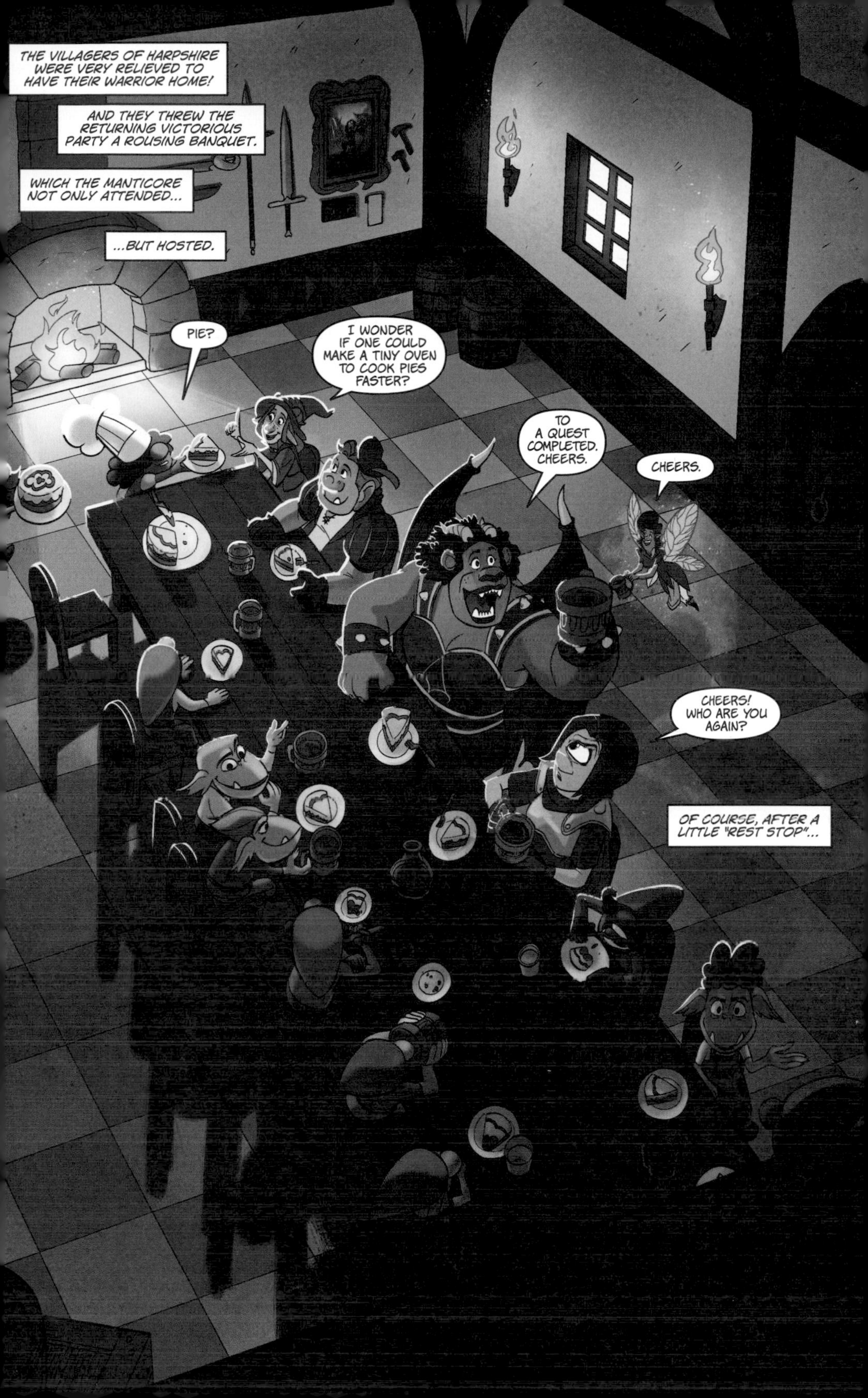
THE VILLAGERS OF HARPSHIRE WERE VERY RELIEVED TO HAVE THEIR WARRIOR HOME!
AND THEY THREW THE RETURNING VICTORIOUS PARTY A ROUSING BANQUET.
WHICH THE MANTICORE NOT ONLY ATTENDED...
...BUT HOSTED.
PIE?
I WONDER IF ONE COULD MAKE A TINY OVEN TO COOK PIES FASTER?
TO A QUEST COMPLETED. CHEERS.
CHEERS.
CHEERS! WHO ARE YOU AGAIN?
OF COURSE, AFTER A LITTLE "REST STOP"...

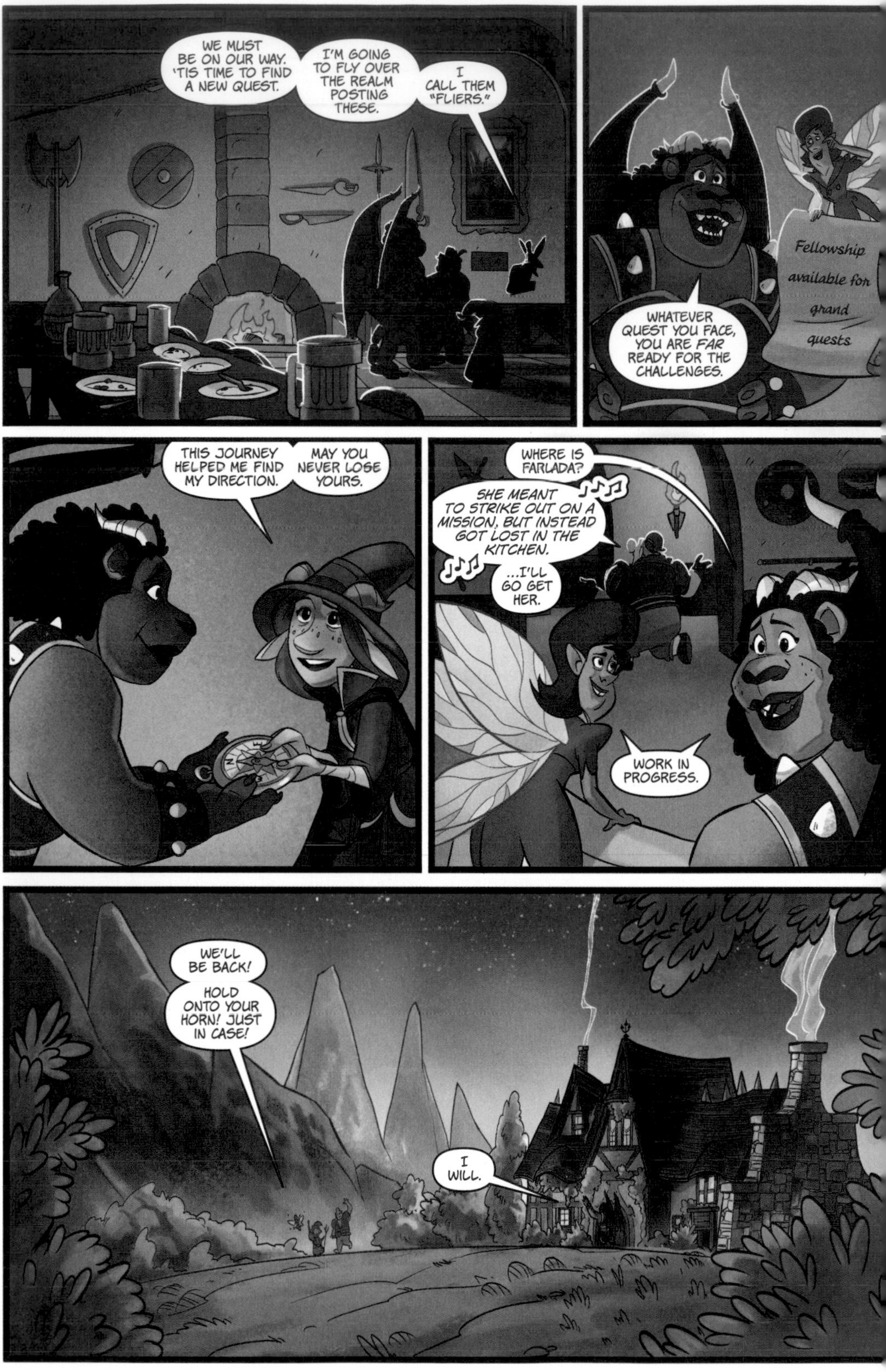

WE MUST BE ON OUR WAY. 'TIS TIME TO FIND A NEW QUEST.
I'M GOING TO FLY OVER THE REALM POSTING THESE.
I CALL THEM "FLIERS."
Fellowship available for grand quests
WHATEVER QUEST YOU FACE, YOU ARE *FAR* READY FOR THE CHALLENGES.
THIS JOURNEY HELPED ME FIND MY DIRECTION.
MAY YOU NEVER LOSE YOURS.
WHERE IS FARLADA?
SHE MEANT TO STRIKE OUT ON A MISSION, BUT INSTEAD GOT LOST IN THE KITCHEN.
...I'LL GO GET HER.
WORK IN PROGRESS.
WE'LL BE BACK!
HOLD ONTO YOUR HORN! JUST IN CASE!
I WILL.

IF THERE WAS ONE THING THE MANTICORE KNEW ABOUT MANTICORES...

...IT WAS THAT MANTICORES CAN CHANGE.

KNOCK
KNOCK

IS THIS THE HOME OF...THE MANTICORE?

WELL THEN.

OF COURSE, CHANGE IS A LITTLE EASIER WHEN YOU HAVE SOMEONE WHO SEES YOUR POTENTIAL.

Strong and noble adventurer seeks same, for company and quest-related networking, share knowledge, maps, magic, talismans, totems, etc.

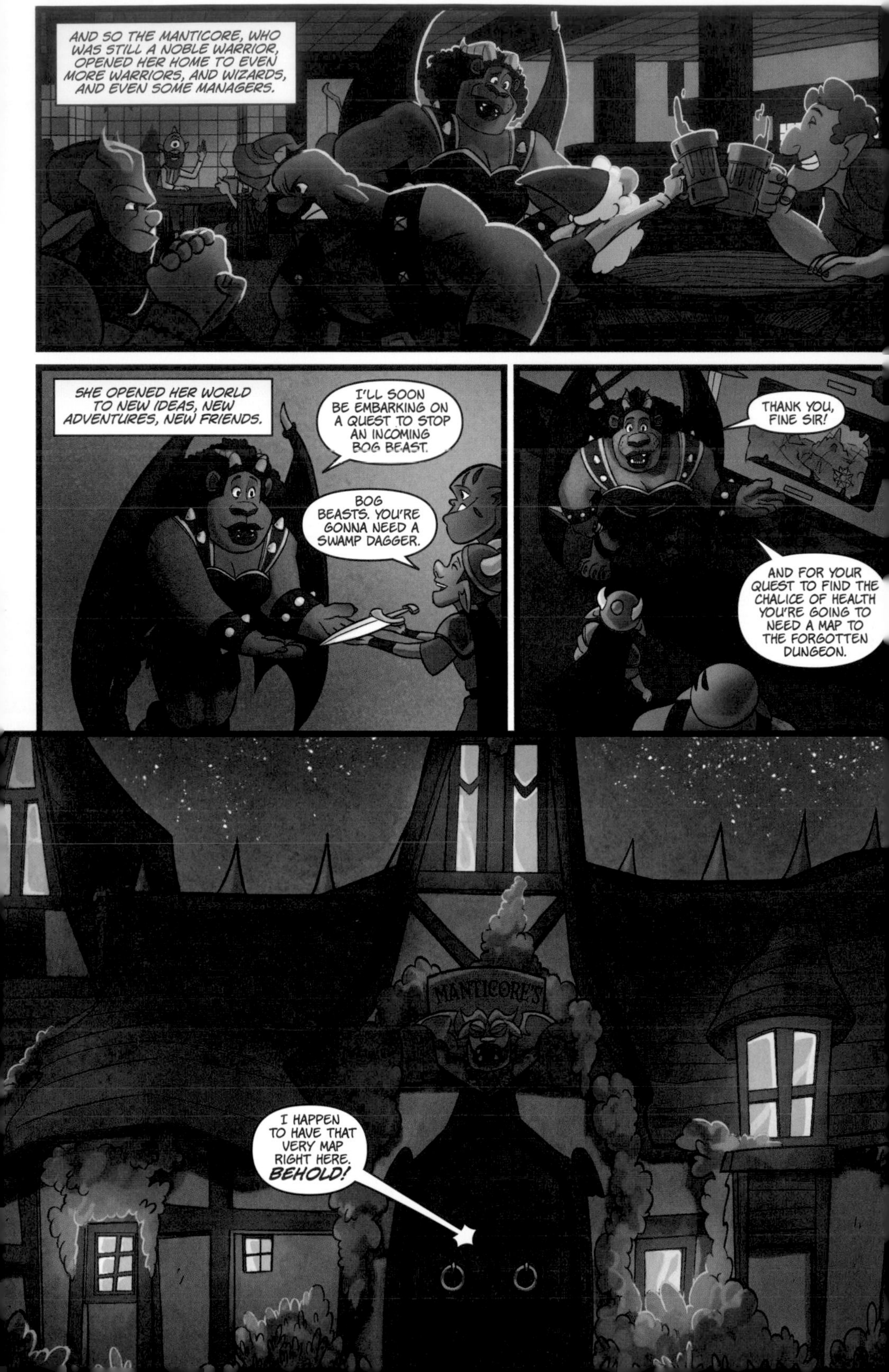

AND SO THE MANTICORE, WHO WAS STILL A NOBLE WARRIOR, OPENED HER HOME TO EVEN MORE WARRIORS, AND WIZARDS, AND EVEN SOME MANAGERS.
SHE OPENED HER WORLD TO NEW IDEAS, NEW ADVENTURES, NEW FRIENDS.
I'LL SOON BE EMBARKING ON A QUEST TO STOP AN INCOMING BOG BEAST.
BOG BEASTS. YOU'RE GONNA NEED A SWAMP DAGGER.
THANK YOU, FINE SIR!
AND FOR YOUR QUEST TO FIND THE CHALICE OF HEALTH YOU'RE GOING TO NEED A MAP TO THE FORGOTTEN DUNGEON.
MANTICORE'S
I HAPPEN TO HAVE THAT VERY MAP RIGHT HERE. BEHOLD!

Disney · PIXAR

ONWARD

SKETCHBOOK

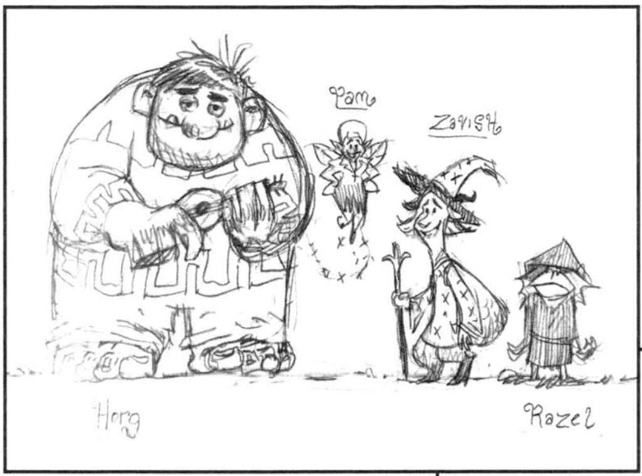

Pam
Zavish
Horg
Razel

Character designs by Dan Scanlon.

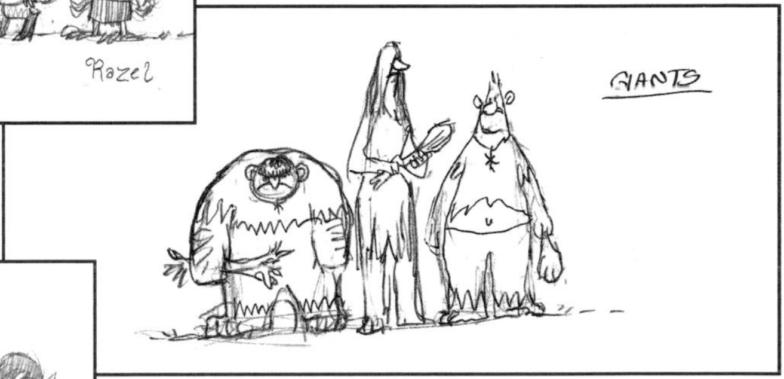

GIANTS

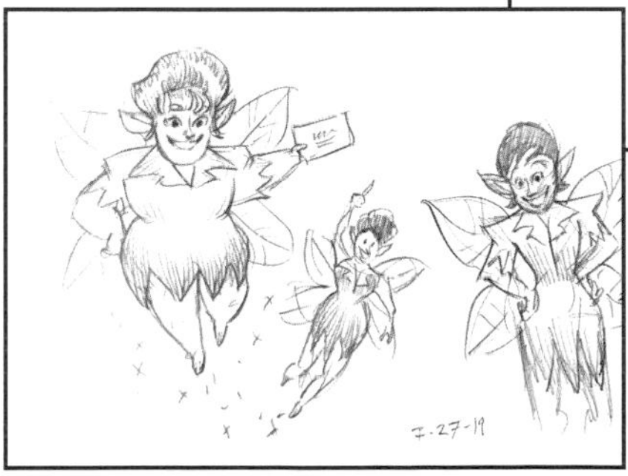

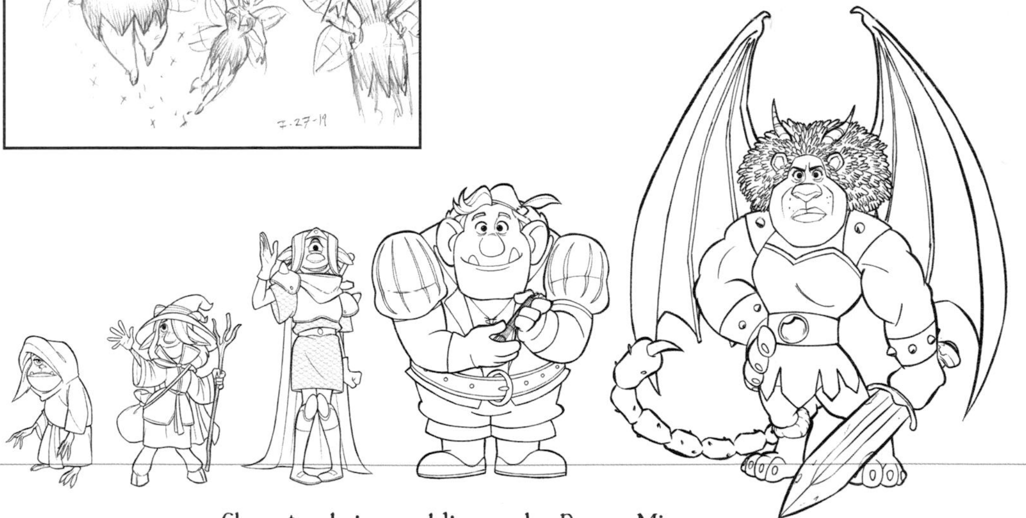

Character design and line-up by Denny Minnone.

STRANGLE WEEDS
SEE SKELETONS OF A FEW
BARD'S & WIZARDS TANGLED
IN VINES.

Page Twenty-Three

Panel 1

Reveal what Zavish is looking at, a ~~massive web stretched between the~~ mountains on either side of the narrow pass the fellowship must pass through, ~~the home of the Montecroy Spiders.~~ ~~It is terrifying.~~ Zavish looks very scared. Horg hugs his lute.

1. Caption: ~~Valley of the Spiders of Montecroy.~~
2. Pam: Okay. Our next challenge! Yes!

Panel 2

Back to the group, Pam gives orders to Zavish, pulling out her spell book, and to Horg as he tunes his lute.

2. Pam: Zavish, prepare your freezing spell.
3. Pam: Horg, a rousing score to lift our spirits.
4. Pam: Manticore...

Panel 3

The Manticore bursts through them, Curse Crusher raised, a warrior rushing into battle. Pam zings out of the way.

3. Manticore: AHHHHH!!!
4. Pam: Uh, Manticore?

Panel 4

The Manticore steps ~~onto the web, sword raised.~~

5. SFX: HISSSSS
6. Manticore: YOU WILL DO NO HARM!

FIGHT!

(top) Dan Scanlon's script notes and storyboarding.

(right) Additional feedback and detail notes from Dan over Mario Del Pennino's art.

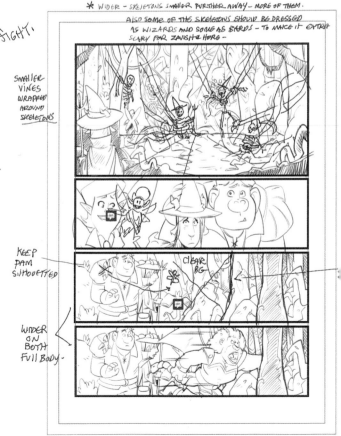

* WIDER - SKELETONS SMALLER FURTHER AWAY - MORE OF THEM.
ALSO SOME OF THE SKELETONS SHOULD BE DRESSED
AS WIZARDS AND SOME AS BARDS - TO MAKE IT EXTRA
SCARY FOR ZAVISH & HORG -

SMALLER
VINES
WRAPPED
AROUND
SKELETONS

KEEP
PAM
SILHOUETTED

CLEAR
BG

WIDER
ON
BOTH
FULL BODY -

23

The process on this graphic novel involved Dan storyboarding parts of the script as inspiration for the interior artists to use. For this particular page (29), artist Mario Del Pennino created a tight pencil sketch using Dan's script notes and sketches. This was then shared with Dan, and he was able to provide additional feedback and added detailing, which Mario included in the final ink stage.

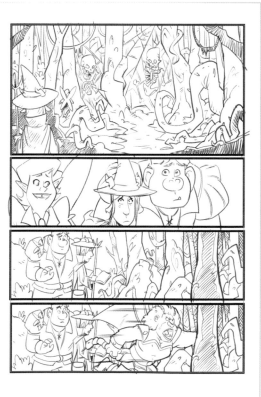

(top) Final inked page by Mario.

(left) Mario's pencils.

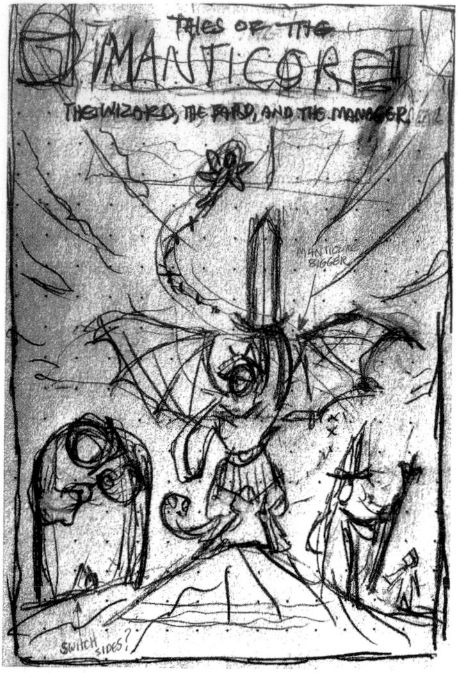
TALES OF THE
MANTICORE
THE WIZARD, THE BARD, AND THE MANAGER
MANTICORE BIGGER
SWITCH SIDES?

Dan Scanlon's original idea for the graphic novel cover.

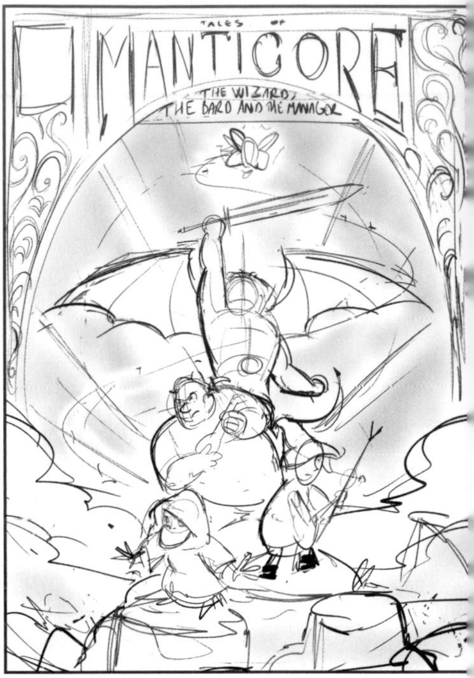
TALES OF
MANTICORE
THE WIZARD, THE BARD AND THE MANAGER

Approved cover sketch from Denny Minnone.

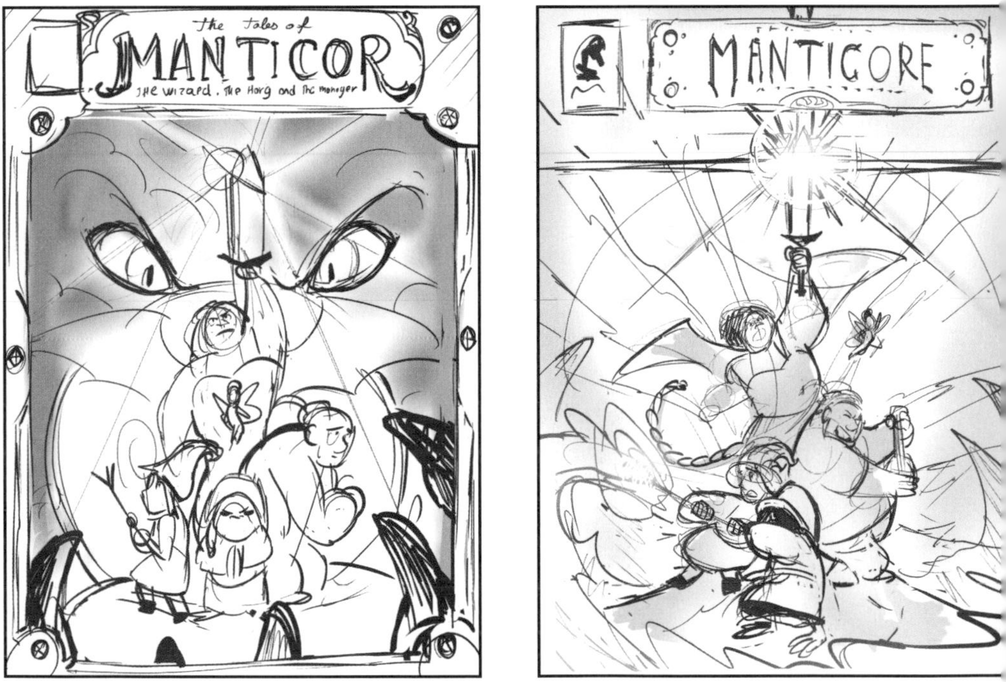
the tales of
MANTICOR
MANTICORE

Additional cover sketches by Denny based off the concept of Dan's cover sketch.

CATCH UP WITH WOODY AND FRIENDS FROM DISNEY•PIXAR'S *TOY STORY*!

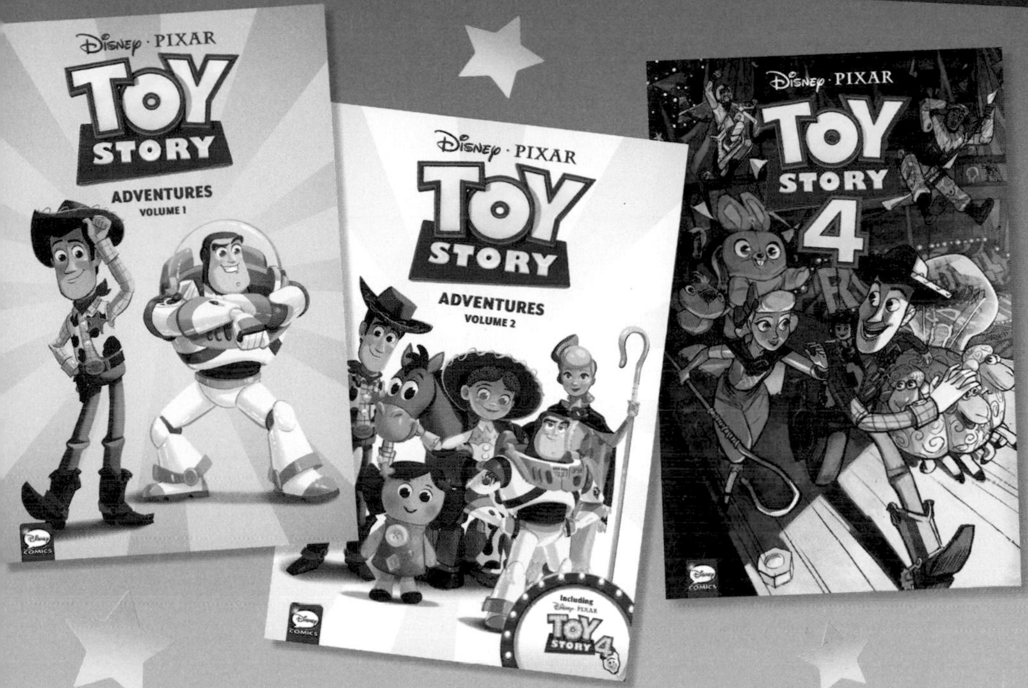
Disney · PIXAR
TOY STORY
ADVENTURES
VOLUME 1
Disney · PIXAR
TOY STORY
ADVENTURES
VOLUME 2
Including Disney · PIXAR TOY STORY 4
Disney · PIXAR
TOY STORY 4

Disney•Pixar Toy Story: Adventures

A collection of short comic stories based on the animated films Disney•Pixar *Toy Story*, *Toy Story 2*, and *Toy Story 3*!

Set your jets for adventure. Join Woody, Buzz, and all of your *Toy Story* favorites in a variety of fun and exciting comic stories. Get ready to play with your favorite toys with Andy and Bonnie, join the toys as they take more journeys to the outside, play make-believe in a world of infinite possibilities, meet new friends, and have a party or two—experience all of this and more!

Volume 1 | 978-1-50671-266-6 | $10.99
Volume 2 | 978-1-50671-451-6 | $10.99

Disney•Pixar Toy Story 4

A graphic novel anthology expanding on the animated blockbuster Disney•Pixar *Toy Story 4*.

Join Woody and the *Toy Story* gang in four connecting stories set before and after Disney•Pixar's *Toy Story 4*.

978-1-50671-265-9 | $10.99

AVAILABLE AT YOUR LOCAL COMICS SHOP OR BOOKSTORE!

To find a comics shop in your area, visit **comicshoplocator.com** · For more information or to order direct, visit **DarkHorse.com**

CATCH UP WITH DISNEY•PIXAR'S INCREDIBLES 2!

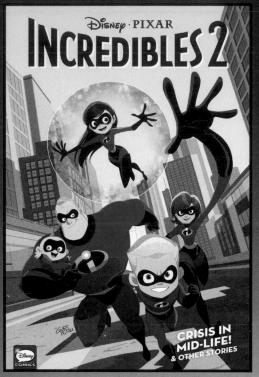

Disney · PIXAR
INCREDIBLES 2
CRISIS IN MID-LIFE! & OTHER STORIES
Disney COMICS

Disney · PIXAR
INCREDIBLES 2
SECRET IDENTITIES
Disney COMICS

Disney · PIXAR INCREDIBLES 2

CRISIS IN MID-LIFE! & OTHER STORIES

An encounter with villain Bomb Voyage inspires Bob to begin training the next generation of Supers, Dash and Violet. Mr. Incredible will find himself needing to pull his family back together . . . because Bomb Voyage is still at large! In another story, Bob tells the kids about a battle from his glory days that seems too amazing to be true—but they never imagined the details would include their mom and dad's super secret first date . . . Finally, in two adventures all his own, baby Jack-Jack and his powers are set to save the day.

978-1-50671-019-8 • $10.99

Disney · PIXAR INCREDIBLES 2

SECRET IDENTITIES

It's tough being a teenager, and on top of that, a teenager with powers! Violet feels out of place at school and doesn't fit in with the kids around her . . . until she meets another girl at school—an outsider with powers, just like her! But when her new friend asks her to keep a secret, Violet is torn between keeping her word and doing what's right.

978-1-50671-392-2 • $10.99

AVAILABLE AT YOUR LOCAL COMICS SHOP OR BOOKSTORE! TO FIND A COMICS SHOP IN YOUR AREA, VISIT COMICSHOPLOCATOR.COM

FOR MORE INFORMATION OR TO ORDER DIRECT, VISIT DARKHORSE.COM